Praise for Peter Sellers

"Peter Sellers is one of Canada's most entertaining short story writers... You'll find yourself laughing even as the shivers crawl up and down your spine."

– Peter Robinson, Arthur Ellis Award-winning author of *Dead Right* and *In a Dry Season*

"One of the key figures in the Canadian mystery renaissance of the '80s and '90s."

– Jon L. Breen, author of *A Shot Rang Out* and *The Gather Place* and "The Jury Box" reviews in *Ellery Queen Mystery Magazine*

"Slick writing sprinkled with grit and a touch of the sinister, Sellers is a true craftsman and his stories are well worth everyone's time."

– J. Kent Messum, Author of *Bait* and *Husk*
Arthur Ellis award winner for Best First Novel

"An esteemed editor of mystery anthologies...Peter Sellers is one of the best known if least prolific of current writers. His rare short stories are always a treat."

– Ellery Queen in *Ellery Queen Mystery Magazine*

THIS ONE'S TROUBLE

Library and Archives Canada Cataloguing in Publication

Sellers, Peter, 1956-, author
This one's trouble / Peter Sellers.

Short stories.
Issued in print and electronic formats.
ISBN 978-1-77161-124-4 (pbk.).-- ISBN 978-1-77161-125-1 (html).--
ISBN 978-1-77161-126-8 (pdf)

I. Title.

PS8581.O8915T45 2015 C813'.54 C2015-903082-X
C2015-903083-8

Pubished by Mosaic Press, Oakville, Ontario, Canada, 2015.
Distributed in the United States by Bookmasters (www.bookmasters.com).
Distributed in the U.K. by Gazelle Book Services (www.gazellebookservices.co.uk).

MOSAIC PRESS, Publishers

Printed and Bound in Canada.
ISBN Paperback 978-1-77161-124-4
ePub 978-1-77161-125-1
ePDF 978-1-77161-126-8

Designed by Eric Normann

We acknowledge the financial support of the Government of Canada through the Canada Book Fund (CBF) for this project.

Nous reconnaissons l'aide financière du gouvernement du Canada par l'entremise du Fonds du livre du Canada (FLC) pour ce projet.

Canadian Heritage Patrimoine canadien

MOSAIC PRESS
1252 Speers Road, Units 1 & 2
Oakville, Ontario L6L 5N9
phone: (905) 825-2130

info@mosaic-press.com

www.mosaic-press.com

VOLUME 3

THIS ONE'S TROUBLE

PETER SELLERS

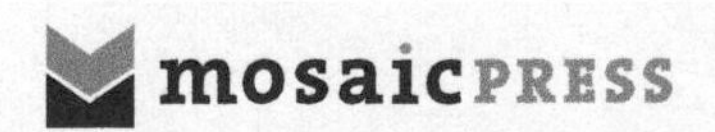

Contents

For Janet Hutchings and Linda Landrigan,
with thanks

Preface

THESE STORIES WERE PUBLISHED BETWEEN 1991 AND 2011. Most of them appeared in either *Ellery Queen* or *Alfred Hitchcock Mystery Magazine*. I was fortunate that both Janet Hutchings and Linda Landrigan, their respective editors, liked my work. The title story was the first to be published, in *Hitchcock* in 1991, and was bought by the late Cathleen Jordan. I owe all three women a great debt.

The biggest fluke was the publication of "Avenging Miriam" in *Queen* in 2001. I almost didn't send it to Janet Hutchings because I never imagined she'd buy it, given its tone and subject matter. But she did, and the story went on to win the EQMM Readers Award that year. That outcome surprised us both.

I would like to thank Matthew Goody for approaching me with the idea of publishing this book, and Howard Aster for a bunch of earlier projects and for recommending me to Matt.

I've made modifications to the stories in order to fix some stylistic issues that I didn't mind when I was younger but that make me cringe now.

Most of these are not conventional crime stories. They are stories about venal behaviour and circumstances that might actually happen in the real world. And the bit about the fat is all true.

Backroom Boys

Originally published in *Ellery Queen Mystery Magazine*, June 2006

AT ONE-THIRTY, AFTER THE BACKROOM HAD CLOSED, KEVIN served us draft beer in coffee cups. We could have drunk from bottles because no cops ever came, but Kevin had been well brought up and liked to break the law discreetly.

The Backroom was a live music club at the rear of an Italian joint on Bloor Street, across the road from the Royal Conservatory of Music. I didn't work there myself. I had a job in a bookstore at Yonge and St. Clair. But I was drinking a fair amount in those days and the Backroom was as good a place as any to do it. The music was okay most of the time. Occasionally Kevin would slip me free food. And it seemed like a good place to meet chicks.

Sometimes, after hours, the musicians would stick around, try out new tunes and tell stories about life on the road. When they talked about the number of girls they'd had I got to wishing I could play an instrument. Unfortunately, I wasn't musical. In Grade Four, when every kid had to be in the choir, the teacher took me aside and told me just to mouth the words.

The musicians would describe gigs they played, from yacht club dances to bars in Northern Ontario with screens in front of the stage to protect them from beer bottles and draft glasses. One balladeer, who sang of peace and romantic love, was booked into such a place by an unhappy accident. When the bottles wouldn't reach him, the locals pressed their faces against the screen and spat.

"Thank you," he'd say after each booed song. "I'm so glad you liked that one. Here's another new tune you might enjoy."

Kevin had run the Backroom since spring. He had made the leap from waiter to manager on the strength of one stroke of good fortune. His girlfriend had previously gone out with the piano player for the band Jerry Spoon and the Tectonic Plates. The Plates played three nights a week at the Victoria Hotel, a rundown dive at Queen and Soho. Every night, the residents of the hotel sat at a round table in front of the stage getting drunk and noisy. The rest of the crowd was loud and mostly pissed and the owner, a former CFL fullback, kept in shape by physically throwing out the most rowdy. Jerry and the band wanted a better gig. Kevin saw his chance.

The Backroom's music budget was four hundred bucks a week. For one guy and a guitar, that wasn't bad. For a five-piece band, it was laughable, even in 1977. But Jerry and the boys were so anxious to get out of the Victoria that they took the offer with little haggling. The usual working week was Tuesday to Saturday, four sets a night, from nine to one. The Plates wouldn't play Tuesday and they got all the food and beer they could consume. That was sure to add up to more than four hundred dollars, but Kevin figured it was worth it.

From the first Wednesday night, the Backroom was jammed. Spoon and the Plates drew students from University of Toronto residences and from the Frat Houses of the Annex, all within easy crawling distance. There was no cover and the beer prices weren't bad.

That week the owners made more money than they ever had in one week before. They thanked Kevin by telling him to make sure it continued.

The first thing he did was to offer the Plates two more weeks. Over the previous seven days, Jerry had become a shrewder businessman. The band agreed, for eight hundred a week.

With the success of the Plates, people started paying attention to the Backroom. Singers phoned looking for gigs. Kevin didn't have to settle for whoever he could get. He was able to hire some of the brightest lights of the Canadian folk scene. Jackie Washington played the Backroom. So did David Wilcox, Willie P. Bennett and a fourteen-year-old guitar hotshot who had to be smuggled in the back door and who filled the place by word of mouth. He's now a big deal in Nashville.

Kevin would bring in the odd classical player from the Conservatory. There was a wicked lutanist named Geordie; some impressive violin players and the occasional classical guitarist who had chops, but none of them was as good a draw as the folk and blues musicians. The classical players didn't have loyal fans who would come every night and drink too much.

Someone who did have fans was Tom Lieberman.

Tom had been front man for a legendary local rock band that almost made it big. An excellent guitar player with a powerful, quirky voice, he wrote songs that were too offbeat for AM radio. But the group got a lot of local club gigs and for a while was the house band at a strip joint in the days of G-strings and an MC between peelers.

When the band came apart, Tom took up an acoustic guitar and reinvented himself as a folk club and coffeehouse performer. Like the Plates, Tom had a dedicated following. He was also just back in town after eight months in Vancouver. Kevin reasoned that people who hadn't heard Tom for a while would jump at the chance.

Tom had surprised Kevin with his phone call. "This is Lieberman."

Kevin stayed professional. "Uh huh," he said.

"I want to play at your establishment," Tom said. "I understand you pay four hundred dollars. That's fine. Next week suits me."

Kevin had a female duo booked for the following week. I was keen on the tambourine player. "I have something lined up," said Kevin, who was a good friend.

"I'm sure you can be persuasive," Tom replied.

Kevin shifted the duo's booking by giving them a second week and the promise of more time down the road. When he called Tom back to confirm, the singer said, "Good. I'll take cash in advance."

Kevin figured that having Tom on the bill was going to pay off, so he said yes. Knowing that the tambourine player would be around for a second week made me happy too.

• • • •

It was obvious that Tom didn't want to be a singer anymore. His deal called for four sets of at least thirty minutes each. He timed each set to the second. Sometimes he'd check his watch in the middle of a tune, see that his half hour was up, and stop playing. "That's enough of that delightful ditty," he'd say and leave the bandstand.

Behind the bar was a small employees-only parking area with a larger public lot behind it. A low wooden fence divided the two and, on nights when the weather was fine, Tom would perch there between sets and talk if someone else was there, or write if he was alone.

While out west Tom had published a collection of delicate poems called *Lover Man*. Gerald Haney, in the *Toronto Star,* said the book contained "luminous poems of lust and yearning." There was a rave in the *Globe & Mail* and *Now* claimed it was "a profound work of deep insight that stands with the best of Leonard Cohen and Gwendolyn McEwen."

Tom did readings whenever he could, selling copies from the stage. But it was hardly a living. The only other marketable skill he had was making music. So he played as infrequently as he could get away with and still stay fed. Kevin was one of the few people who would give Tom work on his terms.

One night, a woman I had not seen before came in and sat at the table in the corner furthest from the bar. Tom was tuning his guitar and did not notice her, but I did. Even though the corner was dimly lit, I could tell she was good looking. I went over.

"Can I sit here?" I asked.

Her eyes were fixed on Tom. "I'm with the band," she said. I thought she was joking. Friends of band members always sat near the stage. But Tom never had girlfriends or groupies come out when he was playing. He was strictly business.

I looked at Tom, on his stool with a quart of Old Vienna on the floor beside him, as he plucked and bellowed. I looked at the woman again, but the way she was watching Tom told me my prospects were slim. I doubt she noticed when I left.

After the set, I went out back. "There's somebody here to see you," I said to Tom.

"They're all here to see me."

"I don't think she's just anybody." I described her.

"Where is she sitting?" As I told him, he took out a pack of cigarettes and lit one. I looked at my watch. It was time for Tom to go back on. Scrupulous as he was about ending his sets on the dot, he was just as precise about starting on time.

"Coming in?" I asked.

"I'll be along," he said. Ten minutes later, he came in. His next set was subdued, all tender ballads. He hardly spoke. And he kept looking into the far corner of the room, but he wouldn't have made out much. He'd be able to tell if someone was there, but no more. There was nothing to see by then anyway. When I'd come in from the parking lot, she was gone.

The first two nights he played the Backroom, Tom read poetry during his sets. "This ain't a god damn literary salon," one of the owners said to Kevin. "Tell that goofy bastard to kill the lovey-dovey shit and sing."

Surprisingly, Tom obliged. Kevin struck a compromise with him. Other performers sold their homemade cassettes from the stage, so Tom could sell his book. Every night, he'd carve a few minutes out of each short set. "I have copies available for just two dollars and fifty cents. Is it worth it, you ask? Indubitably. This inspiring volume includes words like succulent, evanescent, languid and voluptuous. In fact, reading aloud from this book is guaranteed to get you laid. If it doesn't, my friend, then nothing will except cash money. That's why I'm not permitted to read aloud from my book this evening. The proprietors fear the orgy that is certain to ensue, and the subsequent descent of the morality squad." He'd go on in that manner for three or four minutes before starting another song. He sold a book or two every time.

The week after Tom, the female folk duo came in. I was looking forward to watching Pat, the tambourine player, bang and rattle for two weeks. She had long dark hair and wore flowing ankle length skirts that she made herself out of flamboyant fabrics. She'd sing and shake her head, setting her earrings jingling in time to the music. I was mesmerized. The second night they played, I'd had enough beer to make me relaxed but too much to let me remain cautious. I asked her out. She said no.

When I told Kevin how I had fared he said, "It's those skirts she wears. I bet there's something wrong with her legs."

For the next ten days, I stayed away from the Backroom. I know when I'm not wanted.

Tom was friendly when he wasn't on stage. Out back, between sets, he'd talk about politics, literature and the rise of the philistine.

At the time I wanted to be a writer too, although not a poet. I saw there wasn't much money in that. I wanted to be a novelist. Tom was the only published author I knew so he seemed like a good person to talk to. I worked up the nerve to ask him to look at a manuscript I'd completed.

"I'll take a gander," he said. "Scribble a few notes."

"I'll bring it tomorrow." I wanted to ask him how quickly he'd be able to look at it, as I was young and anxious, but that seemed pushy. Instead, I decided to curry favour. "Can you read me one of your poems?"

"What kind of poetry do you like?" he asked.

In school, teachers had read "The Ancient Mariner" and "Prufrock" and "My Last Duchess" by Browning. Each had been exciting, but I had no idea how to answer him. "All kinds," I said.

He shook his head. "That's not good enough."

"But I don't know."

"That's crap. You do know. You just don't have the guts to say it. You need a definite opinion and you need to be tough enough to stick by it. Here's a poem for you." He took a long drag on his cigarette and then spun it away through the darkness. He breathed in and recited, "If I could take a soft-tipped pen/And gently trace the course of your freckles/From next to next to next/Like numbered dots in a child's puzzle book/They would reveal to me/Not an image of bird in flight or wind blown tree/But instead a richer secret/A chart to the centre of love."

Then the clapping started. It was slow and sarcastic, from the darkness of the public parking lot. The woman from the corner table walked towards us. "How lovely," she said.

"Hello, Debbie," Tom said.

"That was beautiful, Tom." She moved past us and through the back door. As she opened it, framed in the light from inside, I thought again how good looking she was.

I was so used to Tom's perfectly timed sets that, the next night, I knew instantly something was wrong. At nine thirty-five he was still playing. At ten o'clock, too. He played all night, sometimes the same song two or three times. He didn't mention his poetry book. He hardly talked at all. It was almost like a four-hour medley.

Debbie was sitting in her usual seat. She looked at her watch as often as Tom usually checked his.

"When does he take a break?" she asked me.

"I don't know."

"Isn't he violating his contract if he doesn't?" That was unlikely. Usually Tom played so little that he owed the place a few extra tunes.

"I want to talk to the manager," she said.

When I reported this to Kevin he shook his head. "I'm busy," he said.

Around eleven Debbie slipped out. When I left after midnight, she was across the street, watching the front door, partially obscured by a lamppost.

I bought a copy of Tom's book and he signed it for me; the first signed book I ever owned. "Someday you'll know," he wrote. It wasn't warm and friendly, but it also wasn't one of those phony inscriptions you get from authors you've met for ten seconds at a bookstore signing. I still have that book and often I open it at random and read a poem or two. I've done that so much that the binding has come loose.

I watched a group of girls who had come in together and had been nursing beers slowly and laughing. They'd been in the Backroom before and once one of them had smiled at me. She looked like she appreciated poetry and I wanted to see if the seductive power Tom talked about was true. I picked what seemed the ideal poem, drained my beer, and went to their table. "Hi, there," I said.

The girls seemed surprised that I'd approached them. I still think there was a sense of eager anticipation in the air. But, with all of them looking at me, I was struck dumb. So I started reading.

"In silence/From my seat behind the microphone/I watch you/As you watch/For your friend to return/And if he does not/If there is indeed a God/Is there hope/That those eyes would watch for me?"

I gave her a wistful look, figuring she'd take the cue. Instead, they all laughed and started clapping. Other people turned to see what was going on. Then the girl I was interested in held out her hand. I was thrilled. Tom's poem had worked. I reached out towards her but, instead of grasping my fingers, she pressed a quarter into my palm.

One night in mid-September I was out back thinking about school. I'd just started fourth year and I was having trouble seeing the point of it. My second novel was coming along fine. I was pounding out ten pages a day on my Underwood portable. Once I got feedback from Tom, who'd need school?

A car pulled up just over the fence from me in the public lot. Caught by the headlights, I felt exposed and trapped, like a POW slipping under the wire. When the high beams switched on, I held my hand up to shield my eyes. "Jesus." I moved out of the light to the driver's window.

It was a '68 Parisienne convertible, with its long hood, massive V-8 and a trunk you could use to move a living room suite. Debbie was at the wheel.

"What are you doing?" I asked, blinking.

"Looking for Tom," she said.

"He's not here. Not this week. Not next."

I don't think she heard me. She sat staring straight ahead into the pool of light.

• • • •

One Saturday, Tom asked me to drive him home. He'd been storing two boxes of books in a Backroom closet and he wanted to take them. "I may want to take off again for a while," he explained.

"Back out west?"

"Maybe Newfoundland. Maybe the Yukon. I've never been and it's great country for poets."

Tom lived on the second floor of one of the old mansions along Jarvis Street. Once the homes of the local gentry, these stately buildings had been converted to restaurants or rooming houses. I parked out front. While Tom took his guitar, his harmonica case, a set of bongos and a small amplifier out of the back seat, I opened the trunk and picked up the books.

Considering how slim the individual volumes were, two boxes of them added up. I perched the boxes on the rear bumper, bracing them with my leg, while I reached up to shut the trunk. Then I hefted the boxes again and turned toward Tom's house. He was at the front door and had set his guitar and the amplifier down. He was talking to Debbie, who stood to the side of the door, out of the porch light.

"I've missed you, Tom," she said.

"Then you need to work on your aim," he said, with no humour. He spread his arms, still holding the bongos and the harmonicas. "I'm a big target."

"Don't make fun, Tom. Haven't you done enough already?'

"Look, Debbie," he said, "whatever you think I did, it was a long time ago. Let's just get on with who we are and where we're going." His voice was soft, the way you talk to a child or someone who's suicidal.

"You say that, Tom, but you don't move on. What are those?" She pointed at the boxes I was holding, which were growing steadily heavier.

"Tom's book," I said, not realizing it was a rhetorical question.

"You see, Tom, you carry me with you." I was tempted to point out that I was the one doing the carrying, but let it pass. "You know you want me. That's why you took so much of me."

"Look, Debbie," Tom said, "I'm a poet. I take stuff that happens in my life and use it. It's nothing personal. I've done it with my parents, friends, other lovers."

"So raping other people's emotions is okay, as long as you do it often enough? No, Tom. You want me. You need me. Try as hard as you like, you can't give me up." She took a step forward. In the light now, I noticed her freckles. "Why else did you come home from Vancouver?"

Tom took a step back and shook his head. "Look, Debbie," he said again, but added nothing to it.

She took another step forward and this time he stood his ground. "You came back for me."

"No, Debbie. I didn't come back for you. I don't want you. Leave me alone. Please."

She looked shocked and then angry. It was interesting but I really wanted them to stop talking so I could go inside and put the boxes down. My arms were shaking.

"You don't mean that, Tom," Debbie said. "Because if you do it means that you betrayed me. You stole from me." She pointed at the boxes I held. "You stole these from me." She swung her arm down on top of the boxes with surprising force. I tried to hold on, but my grip had already been slipping and the boxes fell to the ground, bursting open.

I almost thanked Debbie for taking the load off me. Then she picked up one of the books and slapped it sharply across Tom's face. She walked away, taking the copy with her.

I gathered up the books and Tom took his gear. "She's had a rough time," he said. "I feel sorry for her."

In his apartment, I put the boxes on the table by the window. There was a hole in the glass, covered with clear packing tape, not yet tinged by sunlight. The hole was jagged, with cracks bleeding out from it, the kind of hole I remembered from childhood, when a ball would go astray.

Tom didn't play the Backroom for two months. Business stayed pretty good even though Kevin booked the odd lame act. One guy set a Panasonic tape recorder on a wooden chair. He hit play and the machine blared out tinny renditions of Tin Pan Alley tunes. The singer slouched at the microphone with his hands in his pockets and sang along. His audiences were thin and inattentive.

Other weeks were better. Ron Nigrini was there around the time that "I'm Easy" was a hit. Kevin got Spoon and the Plates back a couple of times. He experimented with a female blues singer who had some style, and a rockabilly trio that was fine until Thursday night when the bass player arrived too drunk to stand. He lay at the back of the stage hugging his bass and plucking it erratically. The next night, the place was jammed with the curious, hoping for a repeat performance.

No matter who played, Debbie did not show up. Then Kevin got the next call from Tom saying he was available. By the time Tom took the stage, she was back.

"Do me a favour, buddy," Kevin said. "Take this money to Tom?"

"Why doesn't he come get it?" I wasn't keen. My car was in the shop and Tom's apartment wasn't convenient to public transit.

"Don't know."

"It can't wait?"

Kevin knew me. "Be a good chance to ask Tom about your book," he said.

A hardware store truck was pulling up as I reached Tom's building. Maybe they were there to fix the door lock in the lobby. It was still broken, though, so I let myself in.

The staircase had been beautiful once, with intricately carved spindles in the railing. Several were missing now, replaced with unfinished lengths of two-by-two, and yet Tom's building was in better repair than some others in the neighbourhood. The ceiling had ornate plaster flourishes and delicate corner trim and, despite a network of cracks, it was still impressive. The doors were impregnable-looking oak. They had been burnished by time and shone in a way that made me want to let the tips of my fingers linger against the wood, until I came to Tom's.

Someone had carved words into the smooth surface. The letters were large, angry and so deep that it must have taken a lot of strength, and a very sharp blade, to engrave them. "Thief of souls," it said. I knocked reluctantly, with a single knuckle.

"Who is it?" Tom's voice was so soft that I thought I had the wrong apartment.

"Tom?" I sounded as tentative as he did.

"Who wants to know?"

"It's me. Kevin sent your money."

The door opened a crack. Tom peered out and then opened the door slightly wider, holding out his hand.

I gave him the money and gestured at the door. "What the hell is that?"

"A fan letter."

"You know who did it?"

He nodded as he counted.

"Who?" He didn't answer, so I tried, "When?"

"This morning." He started to shut the scarred door.

"It must have taken a long time."

"It took one hour and nine minutes," he said.

"This is Tom's last night," Kevin told me the next evening.

I was shocked. Tom had just started his second set. He seemed the same as every other night. There were ways in which he was a pain in the ass. But the people came to see him and they spent money. I wondered what had happened to get him fired so abruptly. And what about my book?

"Can't you let him finish the week?" I asked.

"It's not my idea," Kevin said. "He was gonna just take off, but he wanted to warn me. He said not to tell anybody. Keep it under your hat."

I was out back when Debbie pulled up. She bathed me in her headlights again, but this time shut them off right away. "Is Tom inside?" she asked.

"Not for long," I said. Kevin's news had me shaky and sad.

"What do you mean?"

"He's leaving." I hadn't meant to say it aloud. I'm still not convinced that I did. It certainly wasn't spoken any louder than a whisper, the kind you say to yourself when you're not quite able to comprehend what you think you've just heard.

Debbie stared at me, head tipped to one side. "Leaving," she said, in that same kind of whisper.

After his third set, I said to Tom, "Have you had a chance to look at my manuscript?"

He snapped his fingers, something he did with authority. "Damn, I've been meaning to give that to you." He opened his guitar case and took out a sheaf of papers held together with an elastic band. "I kinda spilled coffee on it. Sorry. And there's a little jam about page one seventy, one eighty. It has potential." He handed it to me. "There's notes here and there. Let's discuss it after the show." He started for the back door.

I took the manuscript to the best-lighted table. His notes were surprisingly thorough. Some were effusive in their praise. Others pointed out redundancies, ugly metaphors and places where I used too many words. His comments on plot weaknesses and cliched scenes were lucid and clear. Nothing he said was without support and, although I didn't agree with all his remarks, I knew that if I followed his guidelines the work would be better. I was so engrossed that I didn't notice that he was late for the fourth set.

Tom always started on the dot of twelve. At twelve ten, I went outside to look for him. Debbie's Parisienne was still there, now backed into its spot against the fence. She was leaning against the car, smoking, and breathing heavily. The cigarettes were taking their toll. Good, I thought.

"Have you seen Tom?" I asked.

"Why?"

"I wanted to thank him."

"I'll tell him," she said, "when I see him again."

Back inside, Tom's guitar was still on the stage. I knew he wouldn't have left it behind. I went out back again. He still wasn't there, and Debbie's car was gone.

Maybe Tom had decided to quit singing for good. I took the guitar home, sure that one day he'd return and want it back. I've kept it ever since. It's the least I can do.

Warren Road

Originally published in *Alfred Hitchcock Mystery Magazine*, October 2005

ONE OF THE FIRST THINGS I LEARNED ON THE JOB IS THAT rich people are cheap. There was this regular customer who would order a small with four toppings and nothing else: no garlic bread, no salad, no soft drink. That cost four eighty-five, the minimum charge for free delivery. She lived way out on Vesta Drive, in the northwest corner of Forest Hill, a neighbourhood full of large homes and privileged people. A run there could take forty-five minutes, depending on lights and traffic. When you finally got there she'd feel the bottom of the pizza box to make sure it was hot. She'd peek inside to make sure the pizza wasn't stuck to the lid and the toppings hadn't shifted to one side. Then she'd hand you a five and wait for change. Every rich person I delivered to was the same, except for one.

One Thursday, Tom gave me a run to Warren Road, another Forest Hill address. It was late, which made things worse. Early in the evening, the upper crust is tight fisted enough. After midnight, you can bank on getting stiffed. When I got there, the man took the pizza, salad and garlic bread and handed me a twenty.

"Thanks." He started to close the door.

"What about your change?"

"Have a beer on me," he said.

Given that beer was sixty-five cents a bottle at the Horseshoe on Queen West, I could have quite a set-to with eight seventy-five.

I drove back to the pizzeria marvelling at the way people can surprise you.

It was the summer of 1978. I had been canned from my job as a computer operator. The boss objected to things I was doing on the four to midnight shift. I got five hundred bucks severance and a thankful feeling that I wasn't stuck in that crummy place. My friend Kevin was a cook at Señor Pizza. It had a thriving delivery business, and needed drivers willing to use their own vehicles. I went down in my oil burning '73 Vega and got a new job.

Driving pies was a lot more straightforward than trying to keep three mainframes up and chugging. Delivery was a cash business and you got paid at the end of every shift, tax-free. We got a twenty-percent commission on all we delivered, except soft drinks and smokes. This was better than most of my buddies who worked retail for minimum wage. On busy Friday and Saturday nights, a hard working guy could rack up eighty or ninety bucks. Holiday Mondays were good too, with people home from the cottage too tired or too fed up to cook.

There was free food whenever the kitchen made a mistake. I discovered early on that I could tell Sal, Tony or Kevin what mistake I wanted them to make, and they'd oblige as long as I shared.

Before losing his license for blowing over the limit, Tom was Señor Pizza's longest serving driver. "There's a chick in the Annex who never has money on her when she comes to the door," he told us one night. "Truth to tell, she never has anything on. She finds other ways to pay."

"You've delivered to her?" Kevin asked.

"You bet I delivered," Tom said. He tapped the ash off his cigarette. "You too, Gino, right?" Gino nodded.

"What street's she live on?" Kevin asked.

Tom made a show of trying to remember. "Huron maybe. Or Howland or maybe Albany. It's been a while. I can't quite remember. You, Gino?" Gino shook his head.

A call came from the kitchen that the next order was ready and Tom went to get it. "Who's up?" he asked.

"Me," I said.

Looking at the order form he said, "Bedford. *That's* where she is. Doesn't that ring a bell, Gino?" Gino nodded as Tom handed me the order. "This could be your lucky night, lover boy." I tried not to look embarrassed. I needn't have worried. My lucky night came later.

Whether there really was a naked woman somewhere on Bedford Road remained a mystery. I never delivered to her. Neither did Kevin. Neither did anybody else in the time I was working. I did, however, deliver to women who came to the door wearing negligees and to men in loosely tied bathrobes. Customers offered me beers and tokes and invited me to parties. Once a guy answered the door dressed as Tinkerbell. He had on tights, wings, and glittering antennae. When he saw me he gave a squeak, turned and scampered down the hall and around a corner. A moment later a man in a Peter Pan costume came out with my money.

"You have to excuse my friend," he said. "He's a little shy."

Señor Pizza was owned by Midori Takada. What a Japanese woman was doing running an Italian restaurant with a half-Spanish name was beyond me. She had two daughters who helped manage the place. Vanessa was being groomed to take over. Gail had plans to leave the restaurant and travel.

"Where are you going?" I asked her.

"Anywhere."

"When?"

"As soon as I get enough money," she said.

In school, I'd never been good at math, but I prided myself on being able to figure change quickly in my head. I'd take the total of the bill, round it up to the next dollar, and then add on the difference in coins. Say someone handed me a twenty for a twelve sixty-five order. I'd round up to thirteen and subtract from twenty. That gave me seven, and the thirty-five cents was easy to add. Then one night I was off by a dollar and ended up shortchanging a guy.

Driving back to Señor Pizza, I realized what I'd done and it bothered me. On my next run I returned the money. If the guy had been a customer I didn't know I wouldn't have put myself out. But he ordered often and he always tipped well. I didn't want to screw that up by having him think that I ripped him off. The potential consequences weren't worth the buck. I had a longer-term perspective.

The guy was surprised to see me, and more surprised when I explained what had happened and held out a dollar.

"Keep it," he said. "You just earned it."

I was angry driving back. The jerk hadn't even noticed he'd been shortchanged. What kind of idiot is that stupid about his money? He wasted my time going back to see him. It probably cost me another run. When I got back to the restaurant, Tom said, "Hey, mama's boy, you just made a friend."

"What?"

"Some guy called to compliment us on our honest drivers." He shook his head. "What's the world coming to?"

Gail came up to me while I waited for the kitchen to make a mistake on a large with red peppers and sausage. Putting a hand on my arm, she said, "It's good to know there's one trustworthy person in this place." Three nights later I got the first run to Warren Road. Later, I figured that was someone's way of rewarding me.

Gail looked you in the eye when she talked to you. I could hold her gaze for a while, but soon I'd have to glance away. It wasn't that I didn't like looking at her. She was cute and I might have asked her out, if she wasn't the boss's daughter. It was just easier to look at her when she wasn't looking at me.

Even though the drivers were busy most nights, Señor Pizza was not doing well. A year earlier, Midori had moved the business. For years she had operated successfully in a small location with seating for twenty-four and a hopping delivery business. Then she decided to climb up in the world. She bought a building that had housed many restaurants over the years: a steakhouse, a seafood place and a joint with singing waiters. They all failed.

Midori turned the ground floor into a swanky dining room for eighty. The second floor housed her office and a banquet hall, although no banquets were ever booked. And, other than a few evenings shortly after opening, the restaurant was never more than half full.

There were still plenty of deliveries, though, and they supported Midori's white elephant. I don't know about the other drivers, but I was aware that I was helping keep her out of receivership. I knew that she knew it too.

Lack of parking was part of Señor Pizza's problem. There were no lots close by and the few spots on the street were usually taken. Parking was so tight even the drivers had to scramble. Most nights I parked at the Texaco across the road. The gas station owner didn't like it much. He yelled at me, but never did anything else. After he closed at seven, nobody cared.

On Friday, when I walked through the restaurant towards the kitchen, there was a Mariachi band setting up by the front window. The musicians wore sombreros, those short jackets and the pants with lots of shiny buttons. This was the start of Midori's music policy. Vanessa had convinced her that live music would help bring in business. Midori agreed and put Vanessa in charge.

Vanessa was sitting by the phone at the entrance to the kitchen, going through the evening's order slips. "Bring me a Coke," she said as I walked past.

When I gave it to her, she glanced at the glass and handed it back. "Too much ice." As I left with my next order she said, "On your way back pick me up some cigarettes."

"There's plenty by the phone," I pointed out.

"Not my brand," she said, as if I wasn't very bright.

A week later, I was racing up Poplar Plains on my way to Warren Road. There was never much traffic on that street and you could clip along, rolling through stop signs. That night, however, someone suddenly backed out of a driveway. I had to brake hard. The car swerved, I lurched forward, and the order flew off the seat onto the floor.

Swearing, I pulled to the curb and picked up the food. Normally, I wouldn't have worried about whether the toppings had slopped around or not, but this was different since the customer tipped like a maniac. I wiped my hands on my jeans and rearranged a few pieces of pepperoni and some tomato and green pepper. Then I looked at the paper bag that held the salad and garlic bread. It was still stapled shut but the side was ripped open and the foil-wrapped bread had come out. When I picked it up, I knew something was wrong. It wasn't lumpy and hot like a bundle of garlic bread usually is. It was cold and geometric, like a brick. I opened it.

Inside was a stack of bills. I opened the glove compartment and, in the glow of the small bulb, I counted. There was four hundred and twelve dollars. The amount was the same when I counted the bills a second time. What the hell was it doing there? I couldn't think of an answer then. But I could figure that the big tipper knew the money was coming. I wrapped the foil up carefully and hurried to Warren Road. Vanessa wanted me to pick up her dry cleaning on the way back.

When I got to the house and handed over the order, the guy looked at the torn bag. "What happened?" he asked. He was smiling but it was the kind of smile you get from a boss who asks what you're doing, even though he knows damn well.

"Oh, yeah," I said, my story all cued up. "I was in such a hurry to get the food to you, I grabbed the bag a little rough and it ripped." I gave him my most honest smile. "They don't make bags like they used to, I guess."

He nodded and gave me another tip. My mouth was dry when I got into the car. On the way back, I bought a stapler and some paper bags and put them in the glove compartment with my unpaid parking tickets.

Several people were leaving when I walked into the restaurant with Vanessa's plastic bag of dresses over my shoulder. This week's band was some kind of weird jazz combo. It didn't sound much like music, and none of the few patrons was paying attention until a woman let out a braying laugh, and the piano player yelled, "Shut up, Eeyore." The music thing didn't seem to be going so well.

On every trip to Warren Road, I stopped and counted the money. It was never the same amount. One night the package held five hundred and seventeen bucks. Another night, there was three hundred and sixty-seven. The smallest amount was two hundred and ninety-three, and the largest six hundred and twenty-two. Soon the total added up to the down payment for a small house.

In the back of my mind was the thought that I should tell someone. There might be a reward in it. Then again, there might not. And who would I tell anyway? I didn't know what was going on. Maybe it was legit. If it wasn't, maybe I could get nailed as an accomplice. I kept my mouth shut.

"What is this?" Midori waved a bundle of orange papers in one hand, slapping it with the back of the other. "What is this?" She shook the papers in Gail's face.

"I don't know," Gail said. "What is it?"

"It's the flyer," she shrieked. "It's our flyer. No, no! It's not ours. It's a flyer from Señor Pizz!"

The way she said it, with the Asian inflection, almost made me laugh. The anger in her eyes told me that wouldn't be a good career move. Midori handed a flyer to Gail and I peered over her shoulder. The type, in at least twenty-four point, screamed, "Señor Pizz."

"Five thousand of these disgusting things have been sent out. We'll be a laughingstock." She threw the bundle to the floor and stormed to her office.

Gail had nothing to do with the flyers. Vanessa had dealt with the printer and I assumed she'd proofread them. She also arranged to have them distributed. To make Gail feel better, I said, "How much more money do you need before you're out of here?"

Gail looked at me like I'd touched a nerve. She picked up the flyers and tossed them in a wastebasket. I rescued a couple as souvenirs.

As it turned out, the typo was no big deal because the flyers were never delivered. I found a bundle of them on the ground behind a nearby dumpster. On instinct, I climbed up the side of the bin. If any copies at all had been handed out, I'd have been surprised. There were thousands of them in among the garbage and the building waste. Maybe someone had stopped the circulation in time. Later though, as I was sifting through the outgoing mail, I noticed an envelope made out to Elite Distribution. Holding the envelope up to the light showed there was a cheque inside. The address on the envelope was the house on Warren Road. Since Gail took care of mailing the cheques once Midori had signed them, the handwriting on the envelope was hers. All of a sudden, it made sense.

Gail wanted out. Tom needed money. It felt like the kind of thing he would do. If you wanted a cheap stereo without a warranty, or if you wanted some grass or tickets to a Leafs game at a premium, Tom was your man. And, at three bucks an hour, working as dispatcher paid a lot less than he made behind the wheel. He had a wife and two kids. Together, Gail and Tom worked the whole scam, skimming receipts from a cash business and doing everything else they could think of to waste money and help force Midori out of business. And they used me as the errand boy. That way neither of them touched the money once it was outside the store. It ought to have been foolproof, but I was no fool.

Maybe the guy on Warren Road was a pal who was holding the cash for them in exchange for a cut. Or maybe he was someone they owed, a bookie or a dealer. I couldn't have cared less. The only thing that mattered was the cash.

They'd stolen more than seven grand, not counting what was in the packages before I got wise. It was time for a bigger slice for me. After all, what were they going to do? Call the cops?

When I parked the next afternoon, I was able to sneak onto the Texaco lot without being seen. I tucked my car in a corner out of sight of the office. But when I went back to deliver my first order, the owner came outside yelling. As I drove away, he waved his fist. I'd never seen anyone do that before. It was kind of comical and feeble. When I got back, I parked illegally on the street with my flashers going. After seven, I started using the gas station again.

I was too smart to dive into anything blindly. The next time I was dispatched to Warren Road, I stopped and opened the package. There was three hundred and eighty-seven dollars. I took out a two, wrapped the bundle again, put it in a new bag and stapled it.

I figured two bucks was the kind of difference that could easily have been a miscount. If it didn't cause a problem, I'd try something bigger next time. It would be easy enough to wait for a night when the total was six hundred or so, take it all and not go back to work. That would be simple but shortsighted. The money was going out in a steady flow and it would be better if there was some way to skim off an ongoing percentage. After all, I wouldn't have minded moving out of my basement into a nicer apartment.

A week later I realized I was being followed. Normally, when I was driving, I didn't pay much attention to what was behind me. Every so often, when I did something bad, I'd check the rearview for cops. But mostly I focussed straight ahead: where was I going and what was the fastest way to get there?

The only other time I looked back was when I pulled over to count the cash. That night I glanced in the mirror and saw a set of headlights stop half a block behind me. Something told me it wasn't a coincidence. I started to drive again, keeping an eye on the mirror. The headlights followed. I drove a couple of blocks and turned right without signalling. The lights kept after me. I turned to the left and the car followed. Whoever was driving was clumsy. That made it easy.

I worked the timing so I hit an intersection just as the light turned red. I ran it, which was no big deal. But whoever was following me didn't have the heart. I figured he wouldn't but, just in case, I drove a few more blocks before stopping to do the count.

The kitchen ran out of olives. It figured they'd run out of something someday. Ingredient control was pretty casual. And olives weren't such a big deal, not like green pepper or mushrooms. But I'd heard Gail on the phone ordering more a few days before. Two nights later,

I found a receipt in the trash. The olives had arrived and Vanessa had signed for them. But now Sal was announcing that there weren't enough left to top a small.

"Once again an idiot," Midori said to Gail. "This stupidity could cost us business." Then the phone rang and the customer wanted olives. It was the first time they'd been ordered all night. Midori glared at Gail and left the kitchen.

Gail looked so upset that I had to get away from her. I checked the dumpster again. There were three large jars of olives, two broken and one intact. I salvaged the unbroken one. Since the seal was still tight, I decided to do Gail a good turn.

Gail looked unhappy when I showed her the olives. My guess was that she or Tom had pitched them to burn more money. "I don't know if this will do any good," I said, "but I picked up these today for my aunt. She likes to make olive oil. Anyway, I had them in the car and thought you could use them." I held the jar out to her. "I can sell them to you at cost."

A week later, when I was sure I hadn't been followed again, I raised the stakes. At first, I was going to take five dollars, but it seemed more likely that someone would make a ten buck error. Out of the four hundred and forty-two dollars in the package, I figured a sawbuck was no big deal.

Later, when I went to cash out, Tom said, "Good night?"

"Not bad." I always kept a pretty accurate calculation of how much I'd delivered and what my cut would be. That night, I figured on sixty-eight bucks and change.

Tom flipped through the stack of hand-written forms from my deliveries and tapped the amounts into the calculator. "Fifty-eight twenty," he said. I must have looked surprised because he asked, "Doesn't that sound right?'

"I thought it'd be more." Tom used to get me to tell him my notion of the take before he did the totals. I was never off by more than a buck or two.

"Hmmm. Let me try again." He shook his head. "Nope. Fifty-eight twenty."

I started to reach for the receipts but Tom gave me a look that made me rethink that.

"Fifty-eight twenty," he said.

Shit, I thought. "I got a bit of a cold," I said. "It must be fuzzing my brain."

"Yeah," Tom said, counting out my money, "that must be it."

My right rear tire picked up a nail on the way back from an early run. It didn't blow out, but I could feel control slipping away and I fought the wheel. Fortunately, I was only a block from the Texaco. I swung in, parked and opened the hatchback.

Grabbing the tire iron, I loosened the nuts on the bad wheel, then hooked the jack to the rear bumper and started to ratchet the car up. When the tire was clear of the ground, I spun the nuts all the way off, put the spare on and started tightening. It was a bad time for the station owner to give me grief.

I could hear him yelling as I tightened the last nut and began to jack the car back down. He was walking across the lot, talking about cops and having me towed.

"Jesus, man," I yelled back, "I got a flat." I lowered the car.

He was about ten feet away, yelling louder. I needed to give the nuts a final turn, so I waved my arm for him to go away. Without thinking, I waved the arm that held the iron and he must've thought I was swinging at him. He jumped back, screaming at me in a language I didn't understand, but every word sounded like swearing.

I knelt down to finish off the nuts, keeping one eye on him. He jabbed his finger at me and walked away.

I could hear the band before I got to the door. It was a punk rock outfit called Firebug that would have been more at home at a place like the Turning Point. As I walked by the stage the lead singer knocked over a large speaker while screaming about love.

There was something wrong at the restaurant. Tom wasn't joking with me like he used to. Gail, the ingrate, had kept her distance ever since I bailed her out with the olives. And Vanessa was bossing me around more than ever. Get this, do that, bring me the other. Maybe the restaurant was closer to crapping out than I'd expected. The time to do something about the money was now. The business with Tom and my commission told me they weren't careless with dough. Skimming wasn't an option. And when I thought about confronting Tom and Gail and telling them flat out that I wanted a piece of the action, my stomach knotted up and I felt like puking. There was no way around it. I'd have to pick a day when the amount was high and take it.

Vanessa gave me twenty bucks and told me to pick up a couple of bottles of wine for her on my way back from Warren Road. The Señor Pizza cellar wasn't good enough.

I decided this would be the night no matter how much cash was involved. It wouldn't matter if I was followed or not. I was prepared. There was a foil wrapped bundle of bill-sized paper in the glove compartment with the paper bags and the stapler. I'd switch it for the cash, make the delivery, grab the tip and add Vanessa's twenty for good measure.

It was dark in the gas station lot, but I could tell from a distance that there was something wrong with my car. It was sitting low. The passenger side tires were both flat. I put the order down on the roof and went around to the driver's side. Those tires were flat too. They'd been slashed.

Jesus, I thought, who would do that to me? There was no place I knew of to get one tire, let alone four, at that time of night. I'd have to go back and get Tom to pass the order on to someone else and wait for the next opportunity.

I had started back to the restaurant when I saw two men approaching. They were probably looking for a smoke or a handout. I angled away from them. They separated and cut me off.

"That your car?" one of them asked.

"Yeah," I said, looking for a way to get past.

"Too bad about the tires. Good thing you like parking here, 'cause you're going to be here a while."

They were just a few feet away now and they stopped moving. The one who had not yet spoken reached out and took hold of the pizza box, pulling it towards him. "Let me help you with that," he said. I resisted at first, but then it didn't seem wise so I let him take the box.

His friend hit me. He swung unexpectedly and struck the side of my head with his open palm. The blow jerked me to the side, buckling my knees. It was so startling that it didn't hurt at first. Then he grabbed my shoulder and, thinking it was to help keep me from falling, I mumbled, "Thanks." His concern was not for my welfare. Without acknowledging my gratitude, he hit me in the stomach. I doubled over, unable to breathe, and his locked fists struck between my shoulder blades, driving me to my knees. That was it. I may have lifted my arms or thrown a punch in a feeble attempt at protecting myself. If I did, I don't remember.

My attacker knelt down. "If you park here again," he said, "I'll smash your driving foot with a brick. Okay?"

The guy holding the pizza was sniffing the air above the box. "Hey, Bobby," he said, "you hungry?"

Bobby gave me a hard look. "What you got, Jay?'

Jay dropped the paper bag and opened the pizza box. "Looks like tomato, green pepper, pepperoni or salami." I heard a bit of chewing and then, "Yeah, salami."

"Anything to drink?"

Jay set the pizza box down and ripped the bag open. "No drinks," he said. "Looks like a salad and something else." He tossed the salad container off to the side. It soared briefly, then crashed and burst open. He unwrapped the foil package. "Holy shit, Bobby."

"What?"

"Dough. Must be a few hundred bucks."

Bobby walked over, taking the money. "This yours?" he asked me.

I shook my head.

"Mine now," he said. "My guess is, whoever it used to belong to is gonna be pissed. You have a nice day, now." Jay took two slices of pizza, eating as they walked away.

I sat against the car, trying to fill my lungs, wondering what story I could tell Tom that he might believe.

In the Fire

Originally published in *Alfred Hitchcock Mystery Magazine*, July/August, 2005

SHORTLY BEFORE NOON ON A WARM MONDAY IN LATE June, the Asian Express opened to great fanfare and a waiting line of customers. By the end of the following week we were getting hate mail.

The anonymous letters were on stationery from one of the Provincial Government Ministries a couple of blocks away. The correspondent claimed "the best rats in town wouldn't eat there." That wasn't true. I'd seen them in the alley, making off with our scraps.

Kevin and I had found the job at the University of Toronto Student Employment Office. The posting said that a new fast food restaurant needed staff. The pay was two fifty an hour days, and three bucks nights. The job wasn't what either of us was looking for, but it wasn't as bad as most of the other opportunities advertised. It didn't involve waiting tables, lifting boxes or selling things over the phone. We called and were told to be at an apartment in Thorncliffe Park the next evening at seven.

Donald Chu answered the door wearing a tight-fitting tank top and a Speedo. "Come in," he said. "Come in, please."

At first I thought it was another one of those situations and that the ad had been a ruse. But Donald Chu was smaller than I was, and Kevin was a lot bigger. Unless Chu knew karate, we could take him. When he stepped aside we saw three guys and a girl sitting in his dining room. They were around our age and fully dressed. We joined them.

"It is called Asian Express," Donald Chu said as he walked back and forth, waving his arms, "because everything will be fast. The food will be good Chinese food. Egg roll. Chop suey. Pineapple chicken. The service will be fast, fast. The food will be hot and ready. People will come in and get good food fast and go away and come back tomorrow. There is no other Chinese food in the area, and Chinese food is very, very popular." He was right about that. But he didn't explain why his staff consisted of four Jewish guys, a Greek girl, and me. I wondered if the rest of them knew any more about preparing Chinese food than Kevin and I did.

Training took place over two days during the week before opening. In those few hours we were supposed to learn everything there was to know about running a fast food outlet. Fortunately, there wasn't much actual cooking involved. Most of the food arrived already prepared and frozen in vacuum-sealed plastic bags.

One of Donald's equipment suppliers, a flamboyant man in a felt hat and a camel hair sports jacket despite the heat, talked lovingly about the new *bain marie,* a tank of water kept almost at the boiling point. The frozen plastic bags were suspended in the water for set amounts of time, and the food was supposed to emerge hot and ready to serve. The salesman's pudgy hands caressed the machine tenderly and directed most of his instructions at me.

We learned about the microwave oven. It seemed fantastic that you could pop uncooked food into a cold oven and it would be ready to serve a few minutes later. There was a brief seminar on the deep fryer and how to make egg rolls and wonton. I never got that quite right and they frequently came out soggy.

We learned how the steam table worked and we were shown the trick of spraying the food with water and stirring to give the illusion of freshness. As time went on, we did that a lot.

Donald also showed us how much food to serve in the various Styrofoam containers. The small portions were guaranteed to ensure that customers would be on their way quickly. We were shown where to put the garbage in the side alley, and we were taught how to clean and maintain the machines. That information came late in the day. By then I was having trouble keeping my mind from wandering.

Donald posted the first week's schedule. Kevin and I got some of the night hours. Cary and Moshe got the rest. Ira didn't want to work nights and Donald didn't want Louise doing it. She'd have been quite safe, probably, but no one knew that at the time.

For the first couple of weeks, most of the food was kept in a basement freezer and heated up every morning. As the day progressed, we could replenish as needed. The rice arrived freshly cooked daily, delivered to the side door by two Chinese men, and was placed in the steam table. It needed to be sprayed and stirred most often.

I didn't eat Chinese food, but Kevin said that what we were serving wasn't good. The frozen sauces had odd, artificial flavours. The meat that wasn't gristle was dry. The reheating was inconsistent. Donald didn't seem to notice. He let us open up, get the food ready, and serve it with no supervision. When he did show up, he usually didn't stay long.

One night, two girls came in asking for pineapple chicken. There was none ready, but Kevin and I didn't have the heart to tell them. He said it would be a couple of minutes and I got a package from the freezer and popped it into the microwave.

We chatted with the girls until the oven beeped. The chicken was still frozen. I gave it another couple of minutes, then a couple more. We kept joking but the girls were checking their watches. I took the chicken out and touched a couple of pieces. It was warm enough and the sauce was hot. The girls didn't come back to complain. They never came back to eat again, either.

Those who ate there were tourists who didn't know any better and a small group of hardy souls who came back day after day. One of them gazed around the otherwise empty store and looked sad. "I don't understand it," he said, taking his dollar ninety-five lunch. "This stuff is great. See you tomorrow." True to his word he returned almost daily until the end.

The usual customer response wasn't so kind or so generous. A man who stopped in for an egg roll came back and threw it on the counter. "I can't eat this shit. It's disgusting."

Kevin gazed into the deep fryer. He put his face close to it and sniffed. "Maybe we should clean this," he said.

The humidity in Toronto can get bad in July, but in 1975 it was particularly unkind. Being on Wellesley Street just off Yonge, we did a fair business selling cold drinks to passersby. Quite often one of us would have to go down the basement to replace the tanks of syrup. Other than stirring the rice, there wasn't much else to do. We spent a lot of time leaning on the counter watching the street.

"Rapunzel's at it again," Kevin said.

Across the street, on the second floor, was a bodyrub parlour, which were big in those days. One of the girls was a blonde with long wavy hair. She liked to lean out the window and call to men passing below. Most ignored her. Some yelled back. Occasionally, one would head up the stairs.

"You notice something?" I asked Kevin as two plump, balding men surrendered to Rapunzel's call.

"What?"

"All the guys who go up there are old."

"Yeah," Kevin said.

"I wonder what it's like up there," I said.

"One way to find out," Kevin said. "I'll mind the store."

"I'll think about it," I said.

At the end of the second week, there was still enough business dribbling in to keep Donald's spirits high. But he cut staff. "I have to fire Ira," Donald said. "He's too slow. Here we have to be fast, fast." He slapped the back of one hand against the palm of the other. "And I have to fire Louise. She can't work nights." That was too bad. Louise was cute and I thought she liked me.

Thursday was what Kevin and I called Boys' Night Out. There were several gay bathhouses in the area, and Thursday seemed to be when they were busiest.

Not many of the bathhouse-bound men were in the mood for bad Chinese food. When they went by our window, some peered in but most walked past without a glance.

One man, though, stopped at the window. He was maybe fifty and scruffy. He stared through the glass, not at the menu and the décor, as people did in the daytime. He looked at me. I turned away, then back. He was still staring. I told Kevin I had to get something from the basement. When I came upstairs the man was gone.

One of our regulars was a guy who wore military fatigue trousers and had his hair buzzed. He drifted in one evening and stood at the counter eating chow mein. "Good food," he said. We were grateful and gave him a free drink. He looked surprised when I handed it to him. He said his name was Chuck and he told us about things he ate while on patrol in Vietnam. Compared to roasted rat and raw bamboo shoots, our food may have been okay.

Chuck ate without looking at the food. His head never rested. All the time he talked he looked around. It was disconcerting. Kevin and I both started doing it unconsciously.

"Thanks for the Coke," he said, and walked away, searching.

The food had become better. Donald had changed suppliers, probably too late. Word of mouth spreads fast and I wouldn't have been surprised to see people crossing the street to avoid us.

The frozen food was gone. Instead, the Chinese men who brought the rice filled the steam table with the whole menu, fresh and hot. It looked and smelled fine, at least for the first few hours. Then we sprayed and stirred as much as before. If supplies ran low, we called Donald. We had to let the phone ring twice, hang up and then call again before he'd answer.

The next Thursday night, I was cleaning up some garbage that a couple of drunks had left on the counter when the scruffy man came back. He appeared at the window staring like before. As soon as he knew that I'd seen him, he came in.

"Hi," he said.

Kevin was downstairs changing a soft drink canister. I felt like yelling for him to come back but then thought that was foolish.

"What can I get you?" I asked, smiling to counter the fact that I was backing away. There was a louvred door into the kitchen. It wasn't much, and it was held shut by a simple hook and eye, but I wanted to be behind even that suggestion of security.

"Wait." His voice was plaintive.

"Do you want something?'

He grasped my arm.

I was unsure what to do. I didn't seem to have the strength to pull away. Then Kevin came up the stairs.

"Get out," he said. His voice was soft but he spoke with purpose. "Get out or I'm calling the cops." I heard him lift the receiver.

The grip on my arm tightened until it hurt.

Kevin dialled zero. "Get me the police, please," he said.

The man let go abruptly, walked to the door and blew me a kiss.

"It's okay now," Kevin said. He hung up. "You all right?" he asked. I nodded, but it was a while before I could stop shaking.

"Guys kept trophies," Chuck said. Everyone knows about this now, but it was news to us then and brought with it a thrill of the gruesome and forbidden. "Some guys kept ears. Some guys kept wieners." He nodded in a way that included us as men of the world. "I knew one guy," he chuckled, "who went everybody else one better. He took a face. He sliced all around here." He traced the sides of his head, along his hairline, behind his ears and under his chin where it joined the neck. "Then he peeled it off. Lots of guys wrote home about that one, you bet." He munched away contentedly, eyes scanning. "They shipped that guy home, though." He chuckled again. "Imagine that."

Sometimes the bodyrub girls would come in. They had bought food once early on. Now they only got cold drinks. Sometimes Rapunzel came, but usually it was a stacked brunette who we called Miss Twilly, after a character in a William Goldman novel.

"Business stinks, eh?" she said one afternoon.

I found it hard to talk to her, but Kevin had no problem. "Whatever gives you that idea?" he asked.

She laughed. "I ate here," she said. "You oughta give out a length of plastic tube with every meal."

"How's your business?" Kevin asked. I was aching to know, but never would have brought it up myself.

"Better'n this."

"What's your secret?"

"Come over. We'll show you."

Two days after changing the food, Donald had a terrible idea. "We have to tell everyone that we have new food," he said. "I want to have someone walking around on the street with one of those signs." He indicated his back and front.

"A sandwich board," Kevin said.

"Yes, a sandwich board."

"Well," I said, "there are lots of places that make them. And you can hire some derelict to wear it."

Donald shook his head. "No, no. We are not busy, and I don't have extra money to spend. We will make our own sign, and you have lots of time. One of you will wear it." He smiled, as if assuming we'd appreciate this stroke of genius.

Donald bought two sheets of orange Bristol board, a black marker and some rope. Kevin had the neater printing, so he made the sign. It looked uneven and cheap, but Donald nodded and said, "Excellent. Who wants to wear it?"

Kevin lost the toss. "You want us to walk back and forth in front of the store, right?" he asked hopefully.

"All over," Donald said, waving his arm around his head. "On Yonge Street. At the corner. Up and down. Wherever there are people and traffic."

When Kevin had tied the two pieces of card together and slipped them over his head, I held the door for him. He had to turn sideways to get out. "Good luck, pal," I said. "I'll be thinking of you." He walked towards the corner. Miss Twilly was on the sidewalk, laughing.

Donald had left again, and I started preparing for the lunch trickle. When I looked up from dishing out some fried rice for the only lunch customer yet that day, the scruffy man was standing at the window. I almost didn't recognize him. He was wearing a suit and he had shaved. I was so startled that I returned his stare.

"And some chop suey," the customer said, loudly and slowly, as if I was a moron.

"Oh, right." I dished that up, too. The man was still at the window. Fumbling nervously, I dropped the spoon. I picked it up and was going to scoop out the customer's chicken chow mein when he said, "Hey."

"Oh, right." I tossed the spoon in the sink and got another.

The customer looked at his order suspiciously, but he paid. There was no one else in the store. The man was still at the window. He watched the customer leave then he smiled, winked and walked away too.

When I was sure he was gone, I went to the window to look for Kevin. I wanted him to forget the damn sign and come back. He was halfway to the corner, talking with Miss Twilly who put her hand on his chest.

Donald had taken to coming to the restaurant late at night. A few times, Kevin and I were just about to close when he walked in and told us that he was going to stay open a while longer. By then, some of the food had been sitting since ten in the morning. Even spraying and stirring wasn't going to help it look palatable. Maybe that's why he often wore the Speedo. Maybe he figured it would help bring in customers.

On Wednesday night, Kevin said, "We better find something to put the fat in." The fryer held fifty pounds of the stuff, and the job of cleaning it was overdue. We had to drain the fat last thing at night while it was still hot and let it congeal so we could throw it out in the morning. While I cashed out, Kevin found two round metal containers. "How about these?"

"Perfect," I said. We turned the machine off, pushed a container under each spigot, opened them, and went home.

When I walked in the next morning, Donald was fussing with the steam table. The fat had congealed in the two containers. Kevin arrived and we each picked up one of them.

"You can't throw those out," Donald said. "I need them. Use something else." He left without offering any suggestions. All Kevin and I could find was a green garbage bag that had been used before and didn't look promising, but it was almost opening time.

I took a serving spoon and, while Kevin held the bag open, I lifted the containers, tipped them over and scooped the fat into the bag. The sound was unpleasant.

When the containers were empty, Kevin closed the bag and began dragging it across the kitchen floor. Through a small tear that we hadn't noticed, the bag left behind a six-inch wide trail of slime. Kevin pulled faster. The trail got wider.

I opened the side door so he could back out into the alley. Then I grabbed hold of the bag too. We lifted and, as soon as the bag was clear of the ground, the bottom broke. The fat splatted onto the asphalt and lay wobbling in the morning sun.

"Oh, well," Kevin said. "At least it's outside."

We had to open in fifteen minutes. There was the deep fryer to clean and refill. There were food preparations to make. And now there was a streak of fat on the kitchen floor to clean up.

I had mopped the floor. Kevin had scrubbed the deep fryer, replaced the fat and unlocked the front door. We were watching people pass by, wondering if anyone would come in, when a woman slid off the sidewalk. She had been walking quickly and all of a sudden she looked like someone on skates for the first time. Her feet went in opposite directions, floundering for purchase. She waved her arms in frantic pinwheels. Then she launched off the curb, landing unsteadily in the gutter.

"Wow," Kevin said.

"She's lucky there wasn't a car coming," I said.

The woman looked around with a stunned expression then, gingerly, climbed back onto the sidewalk.

Moments later, a businessman had his feet shoot out from under him, like a silent film character stepping on a banana peel. He twisted his body, arms out for balance, briefcase bursting on the sidewalk. He caught himself awkwardly and froze, as if bracing for an aftershock.

Kevin said, "Oh no." We went to the side door. It was very hot in the alley and the pile of fat was gone.

Kevin lost the toss. Taking a bucket of hot water and a mop, he went out onto Wellesley to clean up the fat. A few more people had done pirouettes in front of the window but no one had been hurt or been crushed by a truck.

When Donald returned, he was pleased to see that we had saved his metal containers. He told us that Moshe had quit. He hadn't taken to wearing the sandwich board as good-naturedly as Kevin. He was a doctor's son.

Being suddenly short of staff, Donald wanted us to work through until two a.m. Kevin negotiated time and a half.

Around eleven p.m., Chuck came in for his chop suey. I gave him a free drink. It was habit now, although he was as surprised and appreciative as he had been the first time.

It was still hot outside and there was no hint that things might cool off. The extra heat from the *bain marie,* the deep fryer and the steam table made it worse. This was a time before every place was air-conditioned. Movie houses still could draw customers by advertising, "It's cool inside."

Chuck didn't mind the heat. He leaned against the counter eating and looking around. "I like this weather. The hotter the better. Stickier the better. Like the jungle."

I wiped the counter as we talked. When I looked up, the scruffy man was outside the window, smiling.

Chuck gave no hint that he'd registered anything, but he must have caught my expression. "Buddy?" He took a large mouthful of chop suey, not looking at the window but obviously seeing it nonetheless.

I shook my head.

"Bad guy?"

"I don't know him."

Chuck turned to look out the window, directly at the man on the other side of the glass. The man stopped smiling and went away.

Just before closing, I took the garbage out to the alley. All I had to do was take two steps outside the door and heave the bag towards the sidewalk. If raccoons or rats didn't get it, the garbage men picked it up sometime after dawn. Just as I was about to swing my arm back to throw, my foot slipped and I almost fell. Damn, I thought, Kevin hadn't cleaned up all the fat out here. I wasn't about to do it now. In the morning I'd slop some hot water around.

After aiming the bag almost perfectly, I turned and saw the body. It was outlined by the glow of the streetlight behind me. At first, I assumed it was one of the bums who slept in the alley some nights. But this one was lying twisted in an odd way. Normally, the bums curled up like babies, even on hot nights.

I wasn't about to touch him. I never disturbed anyone I found sleeping there. But there was an emergency flashlight inside. I switched it on and saw the scruffy man. The ground around his head was bloody, and near his feet it was slick with fat.

He must have slipped and smashed the side of his head, damaging it badly. That was all I could think. I went inside and was going to tell Kevin to call the police but I didn't. It was our carelessness after all. I locked the side door. If the body was still there in the morning, we'd do something.

Chuck had left a short time before and his cup was still on the counter. The ice had melted. I dumped the water in the sink, threw the cup away and headed home.

Blind Side

Originally published in *Alfred Hitchcock Mystery Magazine*, November 2008

IT WAS TUESDAY AND THAT MEANT HUMILIATION. OUR first period in the afternoon was swim. For forty minutes, thirty-five naked boys plunged through the cold water while the teacher patrolled the deck in gym shoes and tracksuit, whistle around his neck.

Nude swimming had always been the policy at the school, a small and elite institution ostensibly for only the most intelligent boys. Fees were low and standards high. Entrance was based on your ability to write a rigorous examination rather than on your father's ability to write a cheque. Held once a year, on a Saturday morning, the exam was taken by hundreds of aspiring geniuses. Few were accepted. My first attempt, for admission in grade seven, was a failure. With hindsight, I should have heeded the augury. Instead, I wrote again, two years later, and gained acceptance for grade nine.

Looking back, it surprises me that no one's parents spoke out against the perversity of forcing their sons to spend a lesson completely naked. Those were the early seventies, however, and parents were more respectful of authority than we are now. Also, for most of the boys, nudity did not matter. But for me, the sole member of my grade who had not reached puberty, every swim class was an exercise in embarrassment.

Until we all stripped together for the first time, I was unaware that I was alone in what I came to view as my mutation. I tried to be discreet, hands placed strategically, back turned as much as possible, but among so many other naked boys there was nowhere to hide. Immediately, there was giggling, pointing and muttering.

Later the words were spoken aloud and boldly. Some of them I knew and others I had not heard before, but their intent to injure was clear. There were vicious and unfounded attacks on my sexual preference. The memory of it still makes my stomach clench.

A few boys did have bathing suits, packed for them by dutiful mothers, but wearing a suit would have caused even more humiliation than exposing my deformity. So, week after week, I endured the torment. Being small, slender and hairless marked me as a weak and easy target who did not fight back.

The worst offenders were Baker and Harley. They seemed too stupid to have gained entrance fairly. It was only after I had been at the school for a while that I understood how helpful it was to have had a father or an elder brother attend. Nepotism paved the way for some of my dimmer classmates.

There were others who joined Baker and Harley in the fun, but in a less systematic way. From Chestechenko, Simons and Crawford there were occasional spontaneous eruptions of brutality. Several others did or said nothing but their silence made them equally culpable.

At my previous school, I had been a popular student. I was chosen among the first for team sports. I was celebrated for my annual contributions to the school public speaking competition—on crowd-pleasing topics such as vampires, ghosts and reincarnation. My description of the eruptions of blood from the body of a staked vampire was received with particular enthusiasm by the students if not by the faculty. In my final year, I was runner-up for the school's Citizenship Award, which was voted on by the students. Frankly, I should have won. To show my commitment to citizenship, I voted for Lynne, the other candidate and the eventual winner. Later, I discovered that she had not reciprocated. That said everything about to whom the prize belonged.

My plunge from the height of popularity to ridicule and abuse was shocking. Had I been the kind of student who had always been despised, it might not have mattered. But to find myself suddenly alone and not merely friendless but surrounded by enemies left me bewildered.

The student body at the school was small: seventy boys in each of grades nine through twelve. However, thirty-five of the boys had begun in grade seven and, by the time the rest of us joined, cliques were firmly established. Some new boys, who were friends of incumbent students, were accepted. Others, who were larger and more confident, also found favour. Those less assertive, and with no one to welcome them, fared less well. By nature, I was not a courageous boy. My mother had pointed this out once, defending me against the accusation of a neighbour. "He's not shy," my mother said. "He's timid."

Eventually, by force of will, I learned to control this flaw. By the time my grade school days drew to a close, I had made myself well-liked. The process, however, had taken years spent with many of the same children. I was unprepared for the reality of a new and unforgiving world.

Having been raised not to make a fuss, it never occurred to me to ask my parents to take me out of the school. That would have necessitated discussing my situation. My father's motto was, "Never complain, never explain." It was easier to endure.

Mr. Trent taught English and had a glass right eye. The real one had been blown out by a land mine during the Second World War. As a result, when he stood facing the class, he could not see the front left desk, closest to the window. This was known as the blind side, and sitting there was always desirable.

On my first day in Mr. Trent's class, he posed a challenge. "If someone had to meet me at a busy train station," he said, "and he'd never seen me before, how would you describe me to him?"

There was silence from the class. There were many things about Mr. Trent that were distinctive. He was short, balding and wore heavy-framed glasses. His nose was large, red and oddly shaped. It had been damaged, we learned later, in the same explosion that cost him his eye and considerable restructuring had been required. Much as we would have done so behind his back, no one wanted to be the first to itemize Mr. Trent's odd characteristics to his damaged face.

"Well, come on," he urged.

One boy put up his hand timidly. "You have glasses," he said.

"Good. What else?"

Another shy voice added, "You have a moustache."

"Yes. And?"

Slowly a few more points came out. Mr. Trent's sparse hair was mentioned, as was his crisp military bearing. Guesses were made as to his height and his age. But the well of details dried up quickly.

Mr. Trent looked at us with curious excitement. "Anything else?" he asked, his voice a parade ground bellow. "Well? Well? What about the eye?" He whipped off his glasses, took a pencil in his free hand and tapped it sharply and repeatedly on his right eyeball. The clicking noise was quite loud, and caused more than one of us to squirm. He did it again, louder. The room was otherwise silent.

"It's glass," he said. "I have a glass eye. Lots of people have moustaches, spectacles and receding hairlines. But not many of us have glass eyes." He said this with pride. "So if you want someone who doesn't know me to recognize me, that's the first thing to mention. Remember that kind of detail in your writing."

It occurred to me to ask if, while waiting to be met, he would stand in the train station tapping his eyeball, but thought better of it.

"I do this every year," Mr. Trent said. "I used to take the eye out and pass it around, but a few years ago a lad threw up and they made me stop." He said this with contempt for both the weakness of that boy and the weakness of the administration.

Mr. Trent is one of the few teachers I remember with fondness. He created in me an excitement for poetry. I can see him still, standing before the class, reading Keats' "On First Looking Into Chapman's Homer". His eye glittered and he pronounced the words with passionate intensity. To this day, I can hear the crisp tee and kay in the poem's final line, "Silent, upon a peak in Darien".

I was not alone in being tortured. There was a small cadre of misfits.

Henry, his face a disaster of pustules, was brilliant and yet so socially inept he seemed brain damaged. In the end, he won a scholarship to MIT and has made a name for himself in the field of pure mathematics.

Kevin and Raymond were more ordinary. Intelligent but non-athletic, their biggest tactical error may have been befriending me. We played bridge together at lunch, with whoever was willing to risk sitting as a fourth.

Then there was Horowitz. He talked a lot about killing. He was obsessed with automatic weapons and explosive devices. He explained in detail what he would do if he could get his hands on some serious military ordnance. Nowadays, he'd be taken out of school and spend his days talking to psychiatrists, but people knew better back then. There had been a photo in the school yearbook showing a blunt-speaking and popular math teacher with the caption, "Sex is like trig. You don't talk about it, you do it". That was how violence was, too. Horowitz, because of his bombast, was not the type to follow through.

"Want to see something cool?" he asked me one day at lunch.

"Sure," I said.

He took me to the auditorium. It would be unheard of now, but under the stage there was a rifle range. Theoretically it was reserved for the cadet corps, but the door wasn't locked so anyone who knew about it could go in.

The rifles stored there had their bolts removed, and there was no ammunition. But everyone knew that the bolts and the bullets were kept in the bottom right hand drawer of Mr. Trent's desk, and neither the drawer nor his office was ever locked.

The cadets put on uniforms and marched around the school parking lot three days a week after class. For more than fifty years, membership in the corps had been mandatory. But, in the late sixties when that requirement had been dropped, enrolment plummeted. Not surprisingly, Horowitz was a cadet.

The rifle range was more brightly lit than I had expected. I'm not sure why I should have been surprised. There is little percentage in shooting at targets that you can't see.

Horowitz opened his briefcase, the solid plastic pseudo-businessman kind with that was known as a browner bag, and removed a bolt and several bullets. He took a rifle, assembled and loaded it. With an enviable casualness, he knelt down and fired three times, in quick succession. Without seeming to aim, he pulverized the heart of the paper target. My ears were ringing. It was so loud I was surprised that the entire school couldn't hear.

"You try," Horowitz said, pinning a new target at the far end of the range and then holding out the weapon.

He showed me how to load it and to line up the sights. I have no idea where my three shots ended up, but they left the target unscathed.

"Do what I do," Horowitz said. "Think of people you hate." It was as close as I ever came to a conversation about life at the school.

Mockery was by no means reserved for the students. There were two Classics teachers at the school. One, who taught both Latin and Greek, was a wheezing, oily man we called Fat Thomas, or Magnus Porcus Gracus. The other one, my Latin teacher, was an elderly gentleman who had been at the school for many years and was known as Uncle Senility. Old fashioned and doddering, he was also the guidance counselor, but the idea of talking to him about anything personal was unthinkable, even less likely than talking to your parents.

Sometimes he was called Uncle Senility to his face. He began every Latin class with an enthusiastic, "Salve, discipuli." Ocassionally, instead of the expected "Salve, magister", the class would reply in unison, "Salve, Uncle Senility." I was never sure if it registered with him or not.

Uncle Senility's apparent lack of awareness helped foster a new trend in my second year at the school. Baker started it, and others followed suit. The school building was old, with large double-hung windows and deep stone ledges. On warm days the windows that ran the length of most classrooms were opened wide. The drapes were drawn back, gathered thickly at each end of the window bank. One afternoon, Baker climbed out onto the window ledge and sat there for Uncle Senility's class, hidden from view by the curtains. There were giggles all round the room but Uncle must have been used to that and, after asking a couple of times, "What's the cause of this mirth, you fellows?" he got on with his lesson. Baker's prank went undetected.

After that, Baker took to sitting on the ledge quite often. It was easy to avoid being caught in Uncle Senility's class and also during English, because the spot on the ledge was squarely on Mr. Trent's blind side.

"Where's Wilkinson?" Uncle might ask, naming a boy who had taken his chance on the ledge. "Not here, eh? Well, tomorrow he'll just have to blunder along in his own ignorance." Uncle Senility was full of such expressions. "Come on, Perkins," he'd say when the class sat stumped by one of his questions, "pull us out of the weeds." It wasn't always Perkins, but he was a particularly inept Latin scholar and thus the preferred choice, which caused Perkins no end of misery.

When any boy did not know and Uncle was feeling puckish he'd force the student to try again in the vain hope that he would stumble upon the answer. "Pull yourself up by your own bootstraps," he would exhort.

These sayings, combined with his tendency to have us sing in Latin songs like "All the Nice Girls Love a Sailor" and a ditty that may have been of his own composition called "Listen Said the Pussy Willow", made Uncle a source of boundless amusement.

A few weeks after my visit to the rifle range, I arrived at school late from a dentist appointment. Walking through the parking lot to the side entrance, I saw Baker perched on the second storey ledge, outside Mr. Trent's class. Stopping, I gazed up at him, wondering if I had time to run inside, take a rifle, and shoot him before the end of class.

Instead, I walked to the doors, directly beneath where Baker sat. He spat. Although I ducked, his saliva hit the back of my neck.

Mr. McIlroy assigned us numerous challenges during swim class. There was the twelve-minute swim, an endurance test where we were graded for how far we could go in the allotted time. This was done either across the pool, with half the class swimming at a time, or lengthwise, with several boys in each lane.

There was the test of treading water for ten minutes at a time, which was easier than swimming. Then there was water polo, an exhausting exercise that gave the larger and stronger boys many chances to elbow you in the face and push your head under with impunity.

The one great gift that the school bestowed on us each year was that we were released early for the summer. While other schools shut down at the end of June, we were free from the beginning of the month.

All summer, I dreaded going back, but I kept my fears to myself. Although I had stopped believing in God long before, I prayed for puberty. But the first wisps, when they finally appeared, were not enough. In September, in an effort to prove that I was not weak and effete, I started riding my bike to school. It took me an hour each way, much of my route along Bloor Street, busy even in those days. It made no difference. No one said anything to me about it but it must have been noticed. I went out one day after school and my bicycle seat was missing. I looked behind cars and in garbage cans, but it was gone. I rode home standing up.

When I got off the subway the next morning, I saw Baker waiting to cross the street. "How was the ride home?" he asked.

My revenge began with the mouse. It seemed a fitting symbol since I was determined to be timid no more. One day, at lunch, I went into our class common room and found it empty. I had slipped away ahead of the rest of my classmates for a few moments of peace. The room was filthy, as usual, used as it was exclusively by teenaged boys and off-limits to the cleaning staff. Eventually, the Headmaster issued an ultimatum that either the room be kept clean or be shut down.

Even by the common room's grim standards, the mouse was something new. When I walked into the empty room, it lay in the middle of the floor, dead from unknown causes and, as soon as I saw it, I knew what I had to do. I took one of the discarded pieces of wax paper that lay about and folded it around the small, stiff body, finishing just as the rest of the boys arrived.

I sat with the bundle in my hand, waiting for one of my enemies to present me with opportunity. No one did right away. They all began eating. Finally, Segal obliged.

I must say that I bore Segal no animosity. He was a benign figure. But his was the only lunch bag available and I did not want to store the mouse in my locker until the following day. When Segal went into the washroom, I slipped the mouse into his lunch bag.

When he came back, Segal reached in and took out a sandwich. He ate it with enthusiasm. I watched him surreptitiously, finding the anticipation hard to control. Reaching into the bag a second time, he drew out the mouse. He looked at the crumpled wax paper and the sloppy folds, so unlike his mother's trim work, and appeared puzzled. Then he unwrapped the paper.

Segal stared down at the mouse with incomprehension and then disgust. He went back to the washroom. When he returned, many boys, including me, were gathered around.

"Who could have done that?" I asked boldly, hoping my triumph did not show.

Segal smiled. "It was my brother," he said, as if with approval. "I put some worms in his lunch last week. I knew he'd get me back. But I never thought it'd be this good." The other boys cheered Segal's brother.

One day, in German class, Baker threw my textbook out the third floor window. He sat beside me and, while Mr. Warfield's back was turned, Baker reached across, took my book and tossed it out.

There was nothing I could do. I couldn't have stopped him without creating a scene. I couldn't ask to go downstairs to get the book because an explanation would have been demanded. Warfield, or Woofy as he was known, would not have believed it. I could not have asked to go to the washroom and come back with the book because that would have required another explanation. It also would have left my other books and papers unguarded and vulnerable.

I sat through the class hoping that my missing textbook would not be noticed. It was, of course. "I trust you are more diligent in your approach to your other classes," Woofy said, eliciting snickers.

After class I went outside and found my book. It had landed on its spine and, being paperbound, had burst apart. The wind had carried off some of the pages. I gathered up what I could, hoping what remained would see me through the year. Textbooks were expensive. My parents had bought them for me and I could not ask for a replacement. In the end, when it became apparent that too much had been lost, I went to the bookstore and got another copy, slipping it in the front of my trousers and leaving the store as innocently as possible.

We were playing floor hockey in the gym. We used hockey sticks with their blades sawn off, and a ring about six inches across, padded with felt, as the puck. You controlled the ring with the tip of your stick.

At one point, I was in the corner with the ring, ready to turn and head for the other team's goal. A boy named Perry was fighting me for possession. He slashed my legs and, in trying to lift my stick, hit my finger sharply. I lifted my stick and let Perry take the ring. He didn't pause to wonder why it was so easy. He took two steps and I ran after him, lowering my shoulder and driving him into the gym wall.

There were few rules in floor hockey, but the one that was sacrosanct was no body checking within three feet of the wall. As soon as Perry's head smacked off the bricks, play stopped. The gym was silent except for Perry's moaning.

Mr. McIlroy pointed at me and shouted, "Go take a shower." It was a relief. I was able to shower privately and without embarrassment. I felt confident that I had made a convincing argument for leaving me alone. It was unfortunate that Perry had been hurt. He was one of the more harmless students, but it couldn't be helped. I had to take every opportunity I could.

On the day my major biology project was due, my father dropped me off at the front door of the school. Usually we both took the subway, but I was carrying the project with me, and it would have been awkward in the crush of the morning commute. He offered to drive me, which was a rare treat. Had he not, I would have gone in one of the school's side doors, as I did every other day.

The project was a large model of a protozoan, made of monofilament, plasticine, toothpicks and balsa wood, mounted on board. It was inside a green garbage bag for protection and had to be held flat, like a tray. By my standards, being an indifferent science student, it was an excellent piece of work. My father, who was much more patient than I, had helped me, and I knew a good mark was assured. When I tried to do tasks like that on my own, such as making the occasional plastic model, the results were messy, askew or broken.

I was walking up the broad steps to the front doors when they opened and Baker came out in company with a gang of boys. Holding my project level before me, I stepped aside to let them pass. As they did, Baker reached out and hit the underside of my project quite hard. It popped out of my grasp, overturned and landed on the concrete steps. There was laughter from the group as they passed, but none of them looked back.

The garbage bag made it impossible to see what damage had been done. Picking the project up, I could feel loose and broken pieces through the plastic. I looked towards the road, but my father had gone.

Uncle Senility called the roll. Baker was among the absent. "Not here again," Uncle mused. "Poor Baker will continue to fall deeper into the pit of ignorance." He called the next boy's name but I could tell by the glances towards the window and the bunched curtains that Baker was on the ledge.

The thought did not occur to me until class was over and I was gathering up my books. I moved slowly, not finished when the other boys began boiling out into the hall. They were all turned from me, surging through the doorway, full of urgency to be at liberty. Uncle Senility had his back to me, too, wiping down the chalkboard on the far wall. As I passed the curtain behind which Baker sat, I put down my briefcase, turned, placed my hands against the fabric, took a breath and prepared to push.

The curtains rustled and a head peered around cautiously, starting at seeing me so close. "I was just checking if it was okay to come in," Wilkinson whispered.

"That's what I came to tell you," I said, pulling my hands back and checking again that Uncle Senility was not watching. "You're safe now."

At some point, Mr. McIlroy decided it would be a good idea for us to do what he called "the Alcatraz swim". His story was that, in attempting to escape from the prison, inmates of Alcatraz would try swimming to shore with their ankles bound and their hands tied behind their backs. How prisoners in such a condition would get to the water's edge in the first place clearly never occurred to us to ask.

The class was split into two groups. The boys in one group had their wrists and ankles bound and were expected, for twelve minutes, to propel themselves up and down the pool with eel-like writhings. Each swimmer had a spotter who followed along on the pool deck, counting every length as it was completed and making sure his swimming partner did not drown. Then the roles were reversed.

When McIlroy assigned partners he did so alphabetically. As a result, Baker and I were together. I tied my own ankles, but there was no option for my wrists. Baker bound them tightly but I determined not to wince.

The swim started at the shallow end. We slipped into the water and began wallowing forward, undulating our bodies. Every time your middle went down and your head rose towards the surface, you gulped in as much air as possible before the movement of your body drove your head back under.

It had not been specified, but it was assumed that we were to swim on our fronts. One boy, known as the Colonel for his dedication to cadets and his military haircut, decided it would be easier to swim on his back. He did so and outpaced everyone else. McIlroy must have noticed what the Colonel was doing, but he said nothing until the twelve minutes were up. Then he told the Colonel that he would have to do it again, the proper way.

The water, full of thrashing boys, was riled and choppy. More than once I took in water, spitting it out as best I could before going under again.

Not trusting Baker to pull me out, I knew that floundering was not an option. I ignored the pain in my wrists, the water in my mouth and the fatigue of my muscles and kept going. Progress was slow but consistent. I kept my own lap count, assuming Baker would either lie about the result or not bother keeping track at all.

When McIlroy finally blew his whistle, boys knelt on the deck and helped their friends out of the water. I didn't bother waiting for help from Baker. I continued into the shallow end and asked another boy to release my hands.

As a young man, my father had sailed on Great Lakes freighters. He had taught me several effective knots. I tied Baker's wrists more securely than necessary. Like me, he had been wise enough to tie his own ankles. At the whistle, he began to heave himself through the water.

Baker was not a strong swimmer. After only three or four minutes, he began to slow. Every time he raised his head to breathe I could sense a desperation that soon escalated to near panic. On the crowded deck, I kept pace with him, counting his increasingly infrequent lengths.

Halfway through the drill, Baker lost the struggle to continue. His feet dropped and he began to thrash in the water. There were so many splashing boys, moving in both directions, that his distress went unnoticed at first by all but me. I watched him with interest as his head slid under and bobbed up again. His squirming did little to keep him afloat. After a few seconds, just before Baker squeaked out a terrified cry, I decided it was best if I seemed to be doing something.

Kneeling on the edge of the pool, I reached out for him but his skin was slippery and he slid away. The other boys had begun to notice and those in the shallow end stopped swimming and stood. Some in deeper water were pulled to the side and held securely by their partners. Baker continued to thrash and bob and wail.

I made a show of leaning out further over the water to grab him. Overbalancing, I toppled into the pool, pushing Baker still further towards the deep end. As I sank, I discreetly grabbed Baker's wrists and pulled him under, too. When I resurfaced, Mr. McIlroy was yelling and there were cries from some of the boys.

Baker was helpless. Mr. McIlroy jumped in with an impressive splash. He grabbed Baker and hauled him to shallow water, lifting him out and placing him on his side on the deck.

Baker retched and water trickled from his mouth. Mr. McIlroy started to untie his hands, struggling with the knot. "Who tied this?" he demanded. I did not answer since the knot had nothing to do with Baker's incompetence in the water.

Baker lay gasping and weeping. I stood staring at him, unembarrassed by my nakedness, and smiled. Mr. McIlroy glared at me, eyes filled with anger. Of more importance to me were Baker's eyes, wide and red and frightened.

Gifts

Originally published in *Blood On The Holly*, Baskerville Books, 2007

BACK IN THE DAYS WHEN YOU WERE STILL ALLOWED TO celebrate Christmas, there were always high banks of snow. There was public carol singing, and the post office delivered Christmas cards in bundles to virtually every home. So many cards were delivered in those days that, for the two weeks leading up to Christmas, students were hired to help the postmen on their rounds. The pay was good, the hours were short and the work was easy. It was ideal. The jobs were coveted. Gerald had university to pay for, and his rent, and he considered himself fortunate to be hired.

Each morning, Gerald went to the postal station. He was assigned to help Old Ben, who had worked the same route for twenty-four years. Ben had bad teeth, gnarled hands and a habit of muttering to himself.

The first morning, Ben gave Gerald his only lesson about delivering mail. They went to the first house together. The letter slot was near the bottom of the front door. Ben handed Gerald a bundle of mail. "Put it through," he said.

Gerald gripped the bundle. As he bent and reached for the letter slot, he could hear Ben muttering beside him. Gerald started pushing the bundle through. Just as his fingers were about to slip into the slot and drop the bundle, Ben grabbed Gerald's wrist and pulled his hand back. "Don't do that."

Ben took the envelopes from Gerald. "Do this." He pushed the front edge of the bundle into the slot, so it was held in place by the spring-loaded flap inside. Then he released his grip, put his palm against the end of bundle and pushed.

The envelopes had gone about half way through when there was a snarling inside the house and the bundle was wrenched forward and out of sight with startling violence.

"Do it the way you were doing it, and you'll lose fingers," Ben said. "I know one carrier lost two. You never know what's on the other side of the door."

"Is there anything else I need to know?" Gerald asked, now the eager student.

"Don't walk across lawns," Ben said. He never did. He would use the walkway to reach the front door, then return to the sidewalk before proceeding to the next house. Never once did Gerald see Ben take a short cut. Gerald was careful not to do so either, unless Ben was out of sight.

Old Ben split the route in two. He took one side of each street and gave Gerald the other. Gerald quickly learned which letter slots to appreciate and which to despise. He liked the big wide ones that opened easily and let you slip even the largest stacks through with no effort. If the slots were chest high, so much the better. He liked capacious mailboxes hung on doors and porch walls. He lifted the lids and deposited the mail with a flourish.

Best of all were the milk boxes, which were always by the side door. In those days, milk trucks still came slowly along the streets, and white-clad men with clinking bottles made house calls.

What Gerald did not like were the old-fashioned, tiny letter slots. They were cramped and mean spirited, forcing him to fold the larger cards and send the envelopes through by twos and threes rather than in bundles. Magazines and catalogues were difficult, too, and he would often hear pages tearing as the flaps inside the slots tore at them. At first he felt badly about this. Then he reasoned that if the people didn't want their mail mangled they should change the kind of letter slot or mailbox they chose to use.

It surprised Gerald to learn that people gave Christmas gifts to the postman. He realized this for the first time when he opened a large mailbox and found a package inside, wrapped in Christmas paper, with Ben's name on the tag. Gerald took the present out and brought it across the street.

Ben held the gift to his ear like a child and shook it. "Chocolates," he said. He shifted the contents of his mailbag and put the package in.

Over the two weeks, Gerald found other gifts. Often, they were bottles. Gerald discovered that Ben's preference was for rye. Gerald made a mental note to buy a mickey to give to Ben on Christmas Eve.

Other people gave Ben money. On a few occasions, Gerald discovered envelopes marked *Ben* or *Postman* in the milk box. When Gerald passed them on, Ben put them in his mailbag, unopened.

Lawrence hated Christmas. He hated the music. He hated the lights and decorations. He hated having to go out and buy gifts for people he didn't like. He hated the forced jollity. Most of all he hated the fact that it was hard to find a card game, and he desperately needed one. George was badgering him for money.

These were the days long before casinos everywhere and online gambling. Had he known what was coming, Lawrence would have been euphoric. But then, on a snowy December day, with Christmas looming, he was broke and in debt and he needed money by Christmas Eve.

The high-stakes games of stud and draw—no one played Texas Hold 'Em then—were illegal and deeply underground. Prior to Christmas, many players were busy with other commitments and the games were fewer. Usually, when he did find one, the other players were as broke and desperate as Lawrence himself. The stakes were low and the chances of winning as much as he needed were slim.

Since it was known that Lawrence had no money, he was not often welcome at the tables where winning would have been profitable enough to make a difference. It was a conspiracy of bastards, Lawrence knew, working together to hold him back.

• • • •

Sometimes, as Gerald was about to put the mail in the letter slot, a front door would open and a woman would appear. They were always holding envelopes and they always said the same thing, "You're not Ben."

"I'm just helping him out until Christmas," Gerald would say. Then, noting the envelope, he would add, "I can take that to him, if you want."

The women always declined, some more graciously than others.

"I'll ask him to come see you," Gerald would offer then. He would cross the street and wait on the sidewalk until Ben came down the walkway. Gerald would name the house in question and Ben would trudge across the road. Gerald always waited discreetly where he was, watching as Ben and the women exchanged brief words and Ben took the envelopes and came back to continue his route.

The finance company was going to take his car. Merry fucking Christmas, Lawrence, he thought. He couldn't let that happen. He needed the car to get to the games, since many of them were a long way from the subway line. He needed the vehicle for more practical purposes as well. It wasn't a good idea to take transit, or walk the streets, with your pockets bulging with cash. And Lawrence knew that he would win large sometime. It was a matter of patience and, if no one stood in his way and did things to hurt his chances, the time would be soon. Also, it was a bad idea to show up at a game without a car. That made you look like a loser.

He had one chance to save the vehicle. He'd been able to browbeat one of the bureaucratic idiots at the finance company into meeting him on Christmas Eve morning. "Be here at eleven," the bureaucrat had said, like a king granting an audience. Lawrence knew he could charm the jerk into leaving the car alone.

The trouble was that now he couldn't go. He'd learned of a card game that was guaranteed to attract some heavy wallets. Lawrence couldn't pass that up. He had to tell his wife that she had to go to the meeting. She had to convince the bureaucrat that Lawrence should keep his car. Lawrence wasn't happy about having to do this. If anyone could screw things up, it was his wife.

Gerald learned early that some people got a lot of Christmas cards, and some people got few. In odd cases, there were houses that received none. This was peculiar in those days, for most neighbourhoods were not as cosmopolitan as they are now. This neighbourhood certainly wasn't. Gerald knew that you would be hard pressed to find a Catholic family, let alone anything more exotic.

There were a small number of homes that only received bills. At least, that's what Gerald assumed from the number of windowed envelopes he put through the letter slots. He felt sorry for these people, except for one household.

Once, as he walked back along the driveway from putting more bills into the milk box, a man came out of the front door. He glared sharply at Gerald, as if knowing what had been brought and blaming Gerald for it. There was so much hate and anger in the glance that Gerald felt chilled. The man, whose name Gerald assumed was Lawrence, got into his car, slammed the door and drove away.

If he's like that all the time, Gerald thought, no wonder no one sends him cards.

"You need to remember what Scrooge said in that movie," George pointed out.

Lawrence was irritated that George had telephoned him at home. "What are you talking about?"

"You know, that movie about Scrooge. They show it every Christmas. On Christmas Eve, when he's leaving work, this guy stops Scrooge and asks for more time to pay back his debt."

Lawrence was puzzled. What did some stupid movie have to do with him?

"Scrooge tells the guy, 'I didn't ask for more time to lend you the money. Why should you ask for more time to pay it back?' You should watch that movie, buddy. There are many lessons you could learn from it." George paused for a moment, as if in thought. "You have to be careful, though. There's a colourized version but it's no good. Don't watch that. The colour looks fake and it wrecks the atmosphere. Be sure you see it in black and white. It's much better."

Lawrence started to protest but George cut him off, "I want that money to buy gifts for my kids. They love Christmas and you're not going to make me let them down. Tell you what, I'll make it easy on you." George adopted an affable manner. "I'll come to your house to pick it up. That's my gift for you. I'll be there Thursday morning at eleven. If someone isn't there to give me the money, it'll go hard for you."

"Where am I going to get that much money by then?" Lawrence was shrill with anxiety.

"Six grand," George said, "on Christmas Eve. Ho ho ho."

It took a lot of effort, but Lawrence managed to scrape together three thousand. Chiselers everywhere were giving him less than he deserved. In the bedroom, he put the bills into an envelope. He took it to his wife.

"A guy named George will be here tomorrow at eleven to pick this up." He described George to her in detail. "Don't give it to anyone else."

"Tomorrow morning?" she said. "I can't..."

"Shut up and do as you're told," he said.

"But you told me..."

"I told you to give this envelope to a guy tomorrow morning. That's all you need to know."

She knew there was no point in persisting. "Where did you get it?" she asked. The sadness in her voice angered him. It was another unfair way she had of making him always feel guilty.

"That's none of your damn business," he said, knowing that, if she wanted to, she could find out soon enough what he had sold this time.

After Lawrence left with the car, his wife was troubled. She saw no way out of the dilemma, no solution that would not raise her husband's ire. She wished she could be in two places at once. She wished she could be anywhere but here. Finally, after spending a considerable time trying to decide which task was more important, she took a sheet of paper and wrote a short note.

Gerald was disappointed that it was his last day. He had come to enjoy the job. The weather appealed to him. True, it was hard on his bare hands and he understood why Ben's were so damaged. Yet he never understood Canadians who complained about the cold and the snow. It made you feel invigorated and alive. He enjoyed the biting wind and the way his nose, cheeks and fingers felt when he was done for the day and was back inside and the warmth returned.

Gerald was surprised when he found the envelope in this particular milk box. He had learned that there was a correlation between how many Christmas cards a household received and whether or not they gave Ben a gift. The Lawrence house seemed to be ignored by everyone except creditors.

Yet here was a white envelope, Christmas card-sized though rather bulkier than usual. There was nothing written on the front, not even the generic *Postman*. Gerald picked it up. It was thick but still flimsy.

At first Gerald thought it must be for someone else but that didn't make sense. After all, the mail was delivered at the same time every day. And, over his two weeks, Gerald had already taken more than a dozen envelopes from mail and milk boxes. Goodness knows how many Ben had found himself. What else could it be but a present left by a homeowner who didn't hold the mailman responsible for what he delivered? Gerald slipped the envelope in his bag. He'd give it to Ben at the end of the block.

Three houses further on, after picking up another envelope, this one addressed to Ben, Gerald took the blank envelope out and felt it again. The thickness puzzled him, as did the lack of a name on the front.

Since there was no addressee, Gerald felt he should be sure before giving it to Ben. Perhaps he'd find some personal item that it would be best to take back. He made a small tear in the corner but couldn't see anything. He decided to open the envelope fully. If it wasn't intended for Ben, Gerald could return it and confess to an honest mistake. No one could take umbrage with that.

Gerald tore along the flap. The contents shocked him. Gerald had never seen so much cash. He riffled the edges of the bills and then, realizing how exposed he was, he stuffed the money back into the envelope and pushed it to the bottom of his bag. He raced to finish the next several houses, not wanting to fall behind.

By the time he and Ben were done the route, Gerald had lost his nerve. He handed over the other envelope and a bottle of liquor he'd collected, both with Ben's name on them. But it felt too late to give him the cash in its torn envelope. How would he explain that he hadn't handed it over right away? Why had he opened it? Why, seeing the cash, hadn't he said anything? Why hadn't he returned it? Why had he taken it in the first place? It was obvious that this could not be intended for a postman. Before putting his mailbag in the trunk of Ben's car for the last time, Gerald slipped the torn envelope into his pocket.

Ben extended his weather-ravaged hand. "Thanks for your help," he said, "and Merry Christmas."

"Thanks, Ben. Merry Christmas to you, too." Gerald produced the mickey of rye he had bought and held it out, feeling it a feeble offering.

The card game did not go well. Lawrence was down when the game broke up early in the evening, three of the players citing Christmas and family and, in one unlikely case, church as lame excuses for leaving. He was angry that they were cheating him out of his chance to get even, let alone get ahead. This was typical. No one gave him the opportunity. Everyone took their turn, and no one gave him his.

When he arrived home, he asked, "Did you give George the money?"

"Yes," she said, but in such a way that Lawrence knew she was lying.

"What did he say?" he asked, his voice rising.

"Nothing," she whispered.

Lawrence knew that it was not like George to say nothing. "What do you mean nothing? Didn't he even say thank you?"

"No. I don't know."

"What do you mean, you don't know? You handed the envelope to him. You must have heard what he said. I know you're stupid, but

I didn't know you're deaf, too." She did not reply and he added, "You did hand it to him, like I told you to."

She shook her head, almost imperceptibly.

"No? Well what did you do with it?"

"I left it in the milk box."

"You did what? I told you to put it in his hands. For Christ sake, can't you follow the simplest instruction? Now he can say he didn't get it and there's no one, not even someone as useless as you, to contradict him."

"I couldn't hand it to him," she said, feeling the beginning of tears. "You told me I had to go to the finance company."

He had forgotten about that. "That's your problem, not mine. You should have planned your day better."

She knew there was no point saying that George must have come to get the envelope, that it was gone and there was nothing to worry about.

"Get into the kitchen," Lawrence said. "You have to learn to do what you're told."

Gerald sat at his table and counted the money again. There was three thousand dollars. It was a remarkable sum and he thought about all he could do with that amount. He could travel, or pay for the rest of his schooling, or possibly even move out of Toronto, to a town where the real estate was cheap, and make a down payment on a small house.

He thought, what a wonderful gift. He wondered who it was really for. Then he set his dreams aside. There was no choice. The money had to be returned. It wouldn't be hard for someone halfway intelligent to figure out who might have taken it. There was too much cash for it to be connected to anything legal.

When Lawrence was a boy, his parents would fill up a stocking for him every Christmas. It always included a book, a chocolate bar, a small toy or two and, tucked down in the toe, there was always an orange. Lawrence hated those oranges. He did not like the taste of them or the smell and, every time he upended his stocking and the orange rolled out, he felt disappointment and anger. Why did they have to give him something he didn't want? Why couldn't he find another toy down there, or more chocolate? It wasn't fair, and as he said his dutiful "thank you" to his mother and father the resentment seethed.

He went into the kitchen and opened the refrigerator. In the crisper he found those same large, thick-skinned oranges. Picking one up, he want to the storage room and found one of the old woolen socks that he and his wife had used for Christmas stockings when the children were small.

As Lawrence walked beck to the kitchen, he dropped the orange into the sock. His wife, standing in the middle of the linoleum floor, looked at the stocking with the swelling in its toe, like a tumour.

"Here's your Christmas gift," Lawrence said. He swung the stocking accurately, the orange pounding heavily into her lower back. She groaned and doubled over. "Stand up," he said. She straightened and he was just about to swing the stocking again when the doorbell rang. At first, he was going to ignore it and continue. Then it occurred to him that perhaps the sound would carry through the door. He did not want anyone to interfere with what he had to do. He handed the stocking to his wife. "Hold this," he said. "Keep quiet, wait here and think about what you have coming."

Lawrence opened the front door and was surprised to see George.

"I am very annoyed with you," George said.

"What?"

"Because of you, I have had to come out here, to a part of the city that I hate, on Christmas Eve. Not once, but twice. And there's no money. My kids are going to be so disappointed."

"What do you mean, no money? My wife left it in the milk box."

"No," George said. "There was this note on the front door, but there was nothing in the milk box." Lawrence read the piece of paper George showed him. In his wife's printing it said, George, look in the milk box. "But there was no money there. There was nothing but a couple of bills. So give me my money now."

Lawrence was stunned. She was ever stupider than he'd imagined. Anyone could have read that note. In his rage he said, "I don't have it, for God's sake. I'm telling you, my wife was supposed to give it to you."

"Don't lie to me," George said, quietly.

"I'm not lying. It's her fault," Lawrence yelled. "She's the one who owes you."

George shook his head sadly. "It's your debt, your responsibility." He shut the door behind him. Then he hit Lawrence in the face.

From the kitchen, Lawrence's wife heard raised voices and then scuffling. There were a few sounds of impact with which she was familiar. Then she heard something falling. Finally, the front door opened and then closed again softly.

After a few moments, when Lawrence did not return to the kitchen, his wife went to the front door. Lawrence lay on the floor writhing. There was blood on his face and the front of his shirt. Spittle frothed at his mouth. His skin had turned an unhealthy colour. His wife noticed more blood and a bit of hair stuck to the wooden frame of the living room door. She realized that he must have swallowed his tongue after falling and that he was choking.

From a first aid course, taken when the children were young, she knew that she should tip Lawrence on his side and ease the tongue free. Instead, she sat on the bottom step, still holding the sock, and watched him patiently.

From two blocks away, Gerald saw the police cars parked in the street and knew he was too late. They had reported the theft. For an instant, he considered walking up to a policeman and turning himself in. Instead, he turned the next corner and went home.

Inside, Lawrence's widow sat on the chesterfield. A policewoman had wrapped a blanket round her shoulders. She put her face in her hands and wept, wondering what she had done to deserve such a gift.

Toothless

Originally published in *Evolve 2: Vampire Stories of the Future Undead*, EDGE Science Fiction and Fantasy Publishing, Inc., 2011

HOT. SUNNY. NO CHANCE OF RAIN EVEN THOUGH IT always felt like I was walking through a fish tank. The same forecast as yesterday. Tomorrow, too, for that matter. They tell me that weathermen used to get it wrong more often than not. Now they're always bang on. Everyone hates people who are right all the time.

I was working days for the third week running. I hated days. Every cop did. Only a few more shifts, though, and then the switch to blessed nights, with temperatures that we'd all conned ourselves into believing were cool.

There were still a few people around who remembered what it was like before the meltdown. Most of them worked in the suicide clinics. If you were feeling down you went in and they'd talk about how it was and show you photographs, or maybe a film. If you were lucky you got slides. Those had the best resolution. After seeing that presentation, most people went out and threw themselves off bridges. A lot of people I used to know had killed themselves but, bad as things were, I figured what came after just might be worse.

I'd heard that once upon a time cities sent out tanker trucks full of water to wash down the roads. That made me shake my head. They tell me it isn't like this in Scandinavia. But I haven't seen for myself, and no one I know can afford the flight either.

When I got off shift I headed to Alan's place. There were eight of us staying there this time. Couch surfing was a way of life for most people those days. The government turned on the air conditioning by zones, one week at a time. So every Sunday morning you saw people clutching toothbrushes and sweat-stained pillows and moving from an apartment in one zone to an apartment in another. Most people had worked out a sharing arrangement among a group large enough to make sure you could sleep with air every day, but not so large as to become unwieldy. Of course, you had to have a couple of spares so you could kick someone out if he became too obnoxious or smelly.

Police work was not about deduction and forensics and solving baffling crimes anymore. Mostly, we protected property: water, zinc and Vitamin D. Zinc was the only thing that really worked to keep the sun from turning you into a walking tumour. Needless to say, it got expensive and that made it a popular item for theft and black market sales.

The meltdown hit everybody hard. But to the biters, it was like a crucifix to the nuts. It took the night away from them. Science is not my strong suit, so I may have got some of this wrong, but here's how I understand it. When the ozone burned up, the radiation that hit the earth pervaded everything. Turns out it wasn't sunlight that made the biters fall apart like lepers on fast forward. It was the radiation, and all of a sudden radiation was everywhere. Even at night, biters were no longer safe. The radiation after dark wasn't strong enough to kill them but it sure made them sick. They went from invincible to weak, ill and tired most of the time. That was no different from the rest of us, of course, but for them it was one hell of a come down. They went from social paragons to pariahs in no time. Needless to say, this decline stripped them of their charisma. There's nothing charming about an emaciated biter bent over, barfing in an alley.

The effect of radiation was combined with the fact that the general quality of available blood was lower. With depleted D levels, human blood was not as nutritious as it had been once and biters began to suffer from malnourishment, too. With their exotic appeal gone, there wasn't much left. Biters weren't used to working for a living and resented having to do it, kind of like exiled royalty. They tended to take a lot of sick time, which made employers frown on them. Some biters took to night jobs like driving cab and waiting tables. A lot of them, though, became hookers, drug mules, petty thieves—anything to find the money to afford the high priced artificial plasma that, like margarine, was not the original but would do in a pinch. From a cop standpoint it was a good thing because there were a lot of snitches around, too. A desperate biter would sell out anybody for a pint.

For those of us who'd spent years exposed to microwaves, phones and iPods, the radiation levels weren't high enough to kill quickly. But during the day, any kind of skin exposure brought up blisters in minutes and tumours shortly after that. It didn't take many of those episodes to add up to bad news.

That morning, we found one of those low rent blood fiends. He was tucked away in a basement that we'd been told was a warehouse for stolen water. That turned out to be untrue. But, in scouting around, Bosco found the body in a dim corner.

"I got something you gotta see," he said.

There was nothing unusual in finding a dead biter. They turned up all the time, OD'd on bad hits of the fake plasma that was always around, cut with cleaning products, melted candle wax or radiator fluid. What made this one different was the blood around its mouth. With biters, there was always some, but this puppy looked like he'd ripped into a full unit of O Positive. "Whose blood is that?"

Bosco reached down and pulled back the upper lip. The absence struck me immediately. "Well, well," I said. The usual startling whiteness was missing. The biter's fangs were gone, by all appearances ripped out by the roots.

"Nasty," I said. "What do you think happened? Bad trick?"

"Gambling debt?" Bosco said.

"In-law trouble?"

Or maybe someone had taken the fangs and was using them on a necklace like people did with shark teeth once upon a time. Neither of us cared. All we had to do was drag the corpse into the sunshine and in a few minutes the problem would disappear. But there was something missing. There was no sign of gear for shooting up. No empty plasma bags. No hint of death by misadventure. When we flipped the body over, just in case he'd fallen on his kit, we saw that his head had been beaten in. That was something new.

Two days later, we found another one. Head bashed in and teeth ripped out. Even though cops weren't called upon to solve homicides anymore, by the time the fourth toothless biter turned up I was starting to sense a pattern.

Our reports were filed. Nobody cared. But the incident nagged at me and I was trying to figure out what the defanging was all about. I ruled out the obvious thoughts right away. Revenge for a child bitten and turned. Revenge for one of the blood infections biters so often spread, despite all the hype about safe biting. None of those felt right.

I went to a peeler bar for a drink. Strip joints had become increasingly popular in recent years. With the necessity of keeping every square inch of skin covered up all the time, the opportunity to glimpse bare flesh in public was precious.

Maybe it was all the toothless biters I'd seen the last few weeks, but I found myself watching the strippers' mouths as they danced, before I looked at anything else. I saw the same thing over and over: a fixed smile, like a rictus. And then one of them flashed something different, a gold tooth. She was leggy and not overly emaciated and her left incisor had been replaced by a golden fang. I knew it couldn't be real, because that baby would have bought enough plasma to feed her for a year. Either that or someone would've killed her and pulled it out of her head, and that would've been a crime that made sense.

"I want to see her," I told the maitre d'.

Guillermo looked doubtful. "There are better," he said. "Much better, special for cops."

"I want to see her. In a private room."

Guillermo opened his mouth and I got the sense that he was going to say something else, but what came out was, "Of course. This way."

I was only alone for a couple of minutes. "What happened to your tooth?" I asked as soon as she closed the curtain. I was never one for prolonged romance.

"You like it?" She touched the tooth with her tongue.

"I don't feel one way or another about it. I just want to know where the old one went."

"Why?"

"Tell me or I'll keep you up past your bed time." Funny that no matter how bad it got for most biters, they always choked on the idea of dying for real. Me, in their situation, I'd be outside waiting for dawn with open arms.

"I lost it," she said.

When she got up off the floor, I asked her again. "Keep lying to me and you'll lose the other one, too."

"I sold it."

"Why?"

"This guy wanted it."

"What guy?"

"I don't know. I never saw him before." That smelled like the truth, although a disappointment.

"You're still doing this, so he can't've paid enough to change your life." I handed her some cash. "Doesn't it affect feeding time?"

"It's like drinking through one straw instead of two. You get to the bottom of the milkshake either way."

Toots was gigging at a basement joint called Bloody Sunday. He was a jazz harmonica player whose teeth gave him distinctive chops. If he hadn't been a plasma junkie he could've been famous. He also knew most of what was going on in the night world.

Toots limped off stage to indifferent applause. The poor quality of his diet had led to rickets. I took out a bag of fine China Red and put it on the table in front of him. "What'll that cost me?" he asked.

"I got your kind turning up with their big teeth ripped out. You hear noise about anything like that?"

"Nothing else done to 'em?"

"Isn't that enough?"

Toots grunted. "There's a rumour. Not saying it's true, but it's what's in the wind. They say someone's collecting teeth and using 'em."

"Using them for what?"

"Grinding 'em up is what I hear."

"Someone's grinding somebody else's teeth. That's a new one. Grinding, like, to powder?"

"So they say. Grind 'em up, mix 'em with blood."

"Why?"

"Don't know more than that. Just that there's a market for fangs. And the lowlifes are on the hunt to collect the bounty."

"Who's paying?"

"Folks I don't wanna meet. That's all I know."

We heard muffled screams, as if from a mouth partially gagged, and moved cautiously towards the noise. One of the first things they taught cops was never to rush in. Most of the time it wasn't worth the effort. Better to get there too late than to wind up in a situation.

Then I started thinking about the fangs and who and why and I started moving quicker than usual. Bosco grabbed my arm. "What're you doing?"

"I want to check this out."

"Let's wait'll it's over."

The screaming was more shrill and insistent. It didn't sound like there was much time. "I'm going now."

"What the hell," Bosco said and, though he sure didn't want to, he followed.

As we went down the alley the screaming grew louder and more agonized. A piercing wail almost made me start to run. Two men held a writhing biter while a third man reached forward with a pair of bloody pliers. There was blood streaming from the biter's mouth and one fang gleaming but only darkness where the other should have been.

"Stop," I yelled. "Police." To make sure they understood, I shot the man who held the pliers. The other two thugs dropped the biter and started to run. Bosco and I shot them, too.

We searched the bodies. The biter was alternately screeching and sobbing. In the pocket of the one with the pliers I found the missing tooth, some cash and a business card. I took them all.

Before we walked away Bosco looked at the biter. "There's nothing we can do for him."

"Put him to sleep," I said.

When I got up the next afternoon, and everyone else in Alan's apartment was gone, I looked at the tooth. I'd never examined a biter fang up close. It smelled slightly rancid and was not as sharp as I expected. But beneath the coating of dried blood, the tooth was the same vivid white as all biter fangs. No matter how bad their health, those teeth never yellowed or decayed.

The cash amounted to all of sixty bucks, just enough for a couple of imported beers. All the business card said was *Clive – Collector* and gave a text address. I sent a message. "Ckng sum 1 2 c my tth."

All the reply said was, "I'll bite", with a time and a street corner.

The car pulled up in front of me right on time. "You got something to show me?" the driver asked.

I held up the fang, shining in the twilight. The car door opened.

The man in the back wore dark glasses and his head was white and smooth. "Show me," he said as the door closed.

I held out the fang again. The man took it between thumb and forefinger. He twisted the tooth around, gazing intently, then, placing it between his teeth, he bit down gently. "Where did you get this?"

"At a crime scene," I said. "I'm a cop. What's going on with these?"

"This was stolen, then, from its previous owner?"

I explained the circumstances and the fang was handed back. "It's a lovely specimen that I would like to have, but I must return it." He reached into his coat pocket and removed a small jar. "All of these have been obtained through legal means."

"Yeah, well, the guy who had your card had just ripped this out of someone else's head, so you may not want to be so trusting in future."

Clive smiled and held the jar up and the teeth inside it shone like precious stones. Shaken, they rattled with a glistening, shimmering sound.

"You bought those? Why?"

"Once upon a time people believed that rhinoceros horn, ground up into powder, could cure impotence. The same was thought to be true of a bear's gall bladder."

"People believe weird shit when they're desperate."

"True enough. However, sometimes folk remedies have substance." Clive shook the jar of teeth once more. "It's amazing how white they stay, no matter what."

They dropped me off a couple of blocks from where they'd picked me up. I had the feeling that he'd told me something significant, but I knew I wasn't getting it. I spent the rest of the night visiting strip clubs and looking for peelers with missing teeth, to no avail.

Two days later I got another message from Clive. We met in the same place as before.

"You were right," he said. "I was too trusting and now I've been robbed."

"That's too bad," I said, "but it happens."

"I want you to find them and retrieve what they stole."

"Why should I?"

"You're a cop," he said and it sounded like he was serious.

"Sorry for laughing but there has to be a better reason than that."

"If you do this, I'll give you something that will change your life." He sounded serious about that, too.

I spent the rest of that night sitting in bars and listening. Thieves tend to have trouble keeping their mouths shut, and when one of them scored off someone as uptown as Clive, silence would be impossible to maintain for long. But I heard nothing until I went back to see Toots.

"I think I got your tooth thing figured out," he said sipping the high-grade synth that I'd slipped him. "Somebody's making sunblock. The best ever. I'd say you hit the streets looking for chicks wearing tank tops."

The only place you saw tank tops these days was in the Museum of Daylight along with the croquet sets and lawn chairs and other relics of more moderate times. If anybody had a secret sunscreen that actually worked he was smart enough to keep it to himself.

"How do you know this?"

"Couple guys shooting their yaps about something they claim they found."

"And it works?"

"Man, they say it works like it's nineteen fifty."

The thieves were not hard to find once we knew what we were looking for. Bosco came with me but I told him nothing. We went to a bar where the two idiots were laughing and shouting.

"What do you want?" one of them demanded.

"We'll discuss that outside." Bosco and I held our weapons.

The thieves reached for their sun gear. "You won't need that," I said.

The taller of the two looked confused. "It's noon, man," he said assuming I was reasonable.

"Too bad for you. But if you're using what you stole, hey, no worries." We pushed them out the door.

The sun hit them like water on the verge of boiling. They whimpered as their skin turned pink and then reddened. We just stood and waited. In minutes, blisters bubbled up on their faces and necks. "Please," the tall one said, eyes closed against the glare. He stopped talking when the sun caught the exposed tip of his tongue. Bending his head down to protect his face, his neck erupted in sores that soon turned black and smelled of roasting flesh.

"Give me what you stole," I said, "and you can go back inside." That was all it took. He reached into his pocket and handed me a small container. Bosco knew better than to ask.

"Thank you," I said. "I'd get that seen to before it turns into something nasty." The two men crawled towards the door of the bar like roaches scuttling for a dark crack.

In the back of his car, Clive opened the container. The ointment was creamy and pink.

"What is it?"

"It's freedom," he told me. "Have you ever felt the sun on your skin?"

"What are you? Nuts?"

"Here," he said, closing the container and handing it back to me. "Try it." He told me what to do and it sounded impossible.

"From blood and fangs?" I asked.

"More or less, if correctly mixed. Try it," he said again. "If you like the results, let me know. We can work something out."

It took a lot of talking to myself before I worked up the guts to do as Clive suggested. Pulling my shirt back from my shoulder, bone white and freckle free, I rubbed on a tiny amount of the cream. I had no idea how much to use but, given the amount of SPF 500 we'd all taken to applying before that stopped working, I went over the area again and again. The cream was slightly gritty when first applied but rubbed in with no trace, no residue, no greasy sheen.

Standing by the door, I took slow deep breaths and then I went out into the sun-battered yard. When I was sure no one was looking I took another breath and peeled back my sun suit, exposing the cream-coated shoulder.

The sunshine felt wonderful, warm but not hot. There were no blisters, black and oozing. Where the sun touched felt so wonderful I almost laughed but caught myself. It was seldom good to be overheard doing that.

Inside, I sent Clive a text. Then I went and bought some pliers.

This One's Trouble

Originally published in *Alfred Hitchcock's Magazine*, July 1991

"I KNOW WHAT YOUR TROUBLE IS," THE SHORT MAN SAID.

At first, Bayly wasn't sure if the guy was talking to him or not so he just sat hunched over his beer staring at the rows of bottles behind the bar.

The short man didn't move. "I know what your trouble is," he said again.

This time, Bayly half turned his head, twisting it a fraction on his cartoon-character neck. The short man stood ten feet away. He was thin and droop shouldered but his suit looked expensive and his hair had that curled perm look that Bayly despised. Bayly turned back to the bottles behind the bar and continued trying to determine whether gin was more popular than vodka.

The short man changed tactics. "Do you know what your trouble is?" he asked, taking the quasi-psychological approach.

Bayly snorted. Sure, he knew what his trouble was. His trouble was that it was the All-Star Break and he was sitting in a bar in Toronto instead of being at the stadium with the American League team, taking batting practice and gearing up for the game. It was due to start soon and Bayly wanted to be good and liquored up before the screen behind the bar was switched on.

His batting average was hovering dangerously close to the Mendoza Line. He was being platooned for the first time in his career. The hometown fans booed when he came to the plate. And his wife had left him two weeks before, because she found out about Janine, and she was after him for a huge settlement. Yeah, Jeff Bayly knew exactly what his trouble was.

"Do you mind if I sit down?" the short man asked.

Bayly hesitated, unsure whether to pound the guy and get it over with. Then he figured that would just compound his problems so he shrugged. The short man sat.

"My name is Henderson." Bayly ignored the narrow hand. "Michael Henderson."

Bayly turned his glance to the short man who returned it with intensity. "I notice that your beer is almost finished. May I buy you another?"

Bayly nodded and the short man signaled the bartender. "Another draft beer for Mr. Bayly," he said, "and a Campari and soda for me, please, barman." The bartender set the drinks in front of them. Henderson perched on a barstool one away from Bayly. He raised his glass and smiled. The red liquid looked like soda pop to Bayly and he felt contempt for any man who would drink it. "Cheers, Mr. Bayly. Here's to your good health and continued success."

"Don't make jokes where the punchline could get you a shot in the mouth," he said.

Henderson shook his head. "I'd be the last one to make jokes at your expense, Mr. Bayly. I'm absolutely sincere. I want to drink to your guaranteed success."

"I've hit three dingers since May and right now I probably couldn't hit a beach ball with a tennis racquet. That ain't my idea of success."

"In baseball terms, no, I'd have to agree with you. But, Mr. Bayly, the tide is about to turn."

Something in the way he said it made Bayly look at him more closely. Henderson was sitting with a studious expression, bright eyes blinking behind his glasses. "What the hell do you mean?"

Henderson lifted a thick briefcase. He set it on the bar and rested his hand on it. "In here," he said in a whisper, "I have the root of your trouble. And in here," he tapped his forehead, "I have the solution." He opened the briefcase to reveal several unmarked videotapes. "It's all on these tapes," he said.

Bayly felt momentary panic as he thought about numerous indiscretions with adoring female fans, but then he remembered that his wife was divorcing him anyway. "What you got?" he asked cautiously.

"I have most of your season here, and some of last year's. In all, over three hundred twenty At Bats. I've studied it for hundreds, if not thousands of hours, and I think I know how we can fix things."

Bayly had heard that before. From the manager, the batting coach, his teammates, from a few hundred fans who'd written in suggesting he do everything from use a lighter bat to jump off the CN Tower. And he'd tried a lot of things too. He'd opened his stance and choked up on the bat. He'd taken a shorter stride for a while and then he'd taken a longer one. He'd switched from one batting glove to two then tried it barehanded. Nothing worked. If anything, the situation just got worse.

"What do you think it is?" Bayly asked, taking another sip of beer.

"It's your left wrist," Henderson said with satisfaction.

"Huh? You mean I'm cocking it too much? Johnny Venuti already told me that one."

"It's not what you're doing with the wrist at the plate. It's what you're not doing in general."

"What the hell does that mean?"

"The bracelet."

At first, Bayly didn't get it. Then it slowly dawned. The bracelet was a huge gold chain he'd worn on his left wrist the first five and a half years of his marriage. His wife had given it to him on their wedding day and he hadn't taken it off, except when he was in bed with other women, until he met Janine toward the end of the previous season. She told him what she thought of jewelry on men.

"I don't know whether it was the weight of that bracelet, the tiny difference it could have made to the timing of your swing, or whether it's just the psychological factor, the way you used to shake it up your wrist before every pitch, but the day you took off that bracelet the wheels came off the wagon, so to speak." Henderson said this as if postulating a scientific theory.

Bayly wasn't much for physics, and he didn't believe that the weight of a hunk of gold could make that much difference. But he was superstitious. He never stepped on the foul line going on or off the field. He took everything out of the on-deck circle before stepping into it. And he always went on to the field before the second baseman and after the right fielder. He believed in what Henderson was saying, but he wasn't about to admit it.

"Where'd you get those tapes?" he asked.

"From the television," Henderson said.

"That's illegal, ain't it?"

"I won't tell if you won't."

They smiled at one another and then the bartender switched on the game. Bayly wasn't half as drunk as he'd hoped to be but as he watched them introduce the starting line-ups, he found he didn't care as much as he had a while earlier. He and Henderson sat watching the game together, not speaking. The bar began to fill up and it was the bottom of the third before Bayly turned to comment on a particularly adept play by the shortstop and realized that Henderson was gone.

A month later, Bayly was on a tear. His average was up 60 points and every time he stood at the plate it looked like the left field fence was only about ten feet away. Pitchers all seemed to be grooving batting practice fastballs right in his wheelhouse. And the team was thriving on it, soaring up the standings so now they were just two games back. But sitting in a bar with four other guys, sucking the foam off an imported draft, Bayly was not a happy man.

He was worried about the next series. Four games at home against the division leaders. Four games that could decide the outcome of the season. Bayly was thinking about those four games, paying little attention to his companions, grunting the occasional uninterested response, when he sensed someone standing next to him.

"I know what your trouble is," a voice said.

"Henderson," Bayly said, turning in his chair. He held up his left hand and shook it, setting the bracelet flapping. "I took your advice."

"So I noticed," Henderson smiled. "But there's something else now, isn't there?"

The other players at the table looked at Henderson with the suspicion athletes usually reserve for outsiders.

"Let's sit over there," Bayly said, picking up his beer and moving to a booth across the room. "Get you a drink? Campari and soda, right?"

When the drink arrived, Henderson said, "There's something else troubling you now, and I know what it is." He tapped the briefcase he again had with him. "In here, I have the root of your problem." He tapped his forehead. "And in here, I have the solution."

"More tapes?"

Henderson nodded. "Of every game you've played in the last two years where Buck Snelgrove was an umpire. He really doesn't seem to get along with you very well, does he Mr. Bayly?"

"That son of a bitch hates my guts."

"Such does seem to be the case. He threw you out of three games last year. Two already this year. And when you come to the plate his strike zone is so big you could drive a truck through it and the wheels wouldn't be called low."

"Damn right." The situation had become so dire for Bayly that every time up he had to swing at almost everything. In his previous game with Snelgrove behind the plate, Bayly had struck out three times. Even being on base did not protect him. Snelgrove called him out on a pick-off when his hand was clearly in under the tag, ending a promising rally amid a chorus of boos.

"And he's behind the plate tomorrow night."

"Yeah. His crew's working the series and that's four games of hell for me. A lot of the players are on edge. This series could turn the season around for us. And winning the first game, man, that's key. But I swear Snelgrove'll kill our chances."

"Perhaps," Henderson said, "and then again..." He let the sentence hang and gave Bayly one of his bright-eyed smiles.

Bayly didn't pursue it further. After a moment he asked, "Why did you come to me about the bracelet?"

Henderson rubbed his jaw. "It's very simple really. I love baseball, have for years. And I admire you as a player. As a child I couldn't play, not well at all. And I'd sit and watch my brothers and the other children running and throwing, hitting, catching. There was something about the game that captivated me. I'd watch every game that came on television. My favourite was Willie Mays, then. I think one always needs a favourite player, like an icon. Over the years, I've had other favourites, they change as careers end and new eras begin. For the past four years, you've been my favourite. Watching you play baseball is almost a religious experience for me. The mighty rip as your bat slices the air is thrilling for me. It's more exciting for me to watch you swing and miss than it is to watch another player hit a grand slam."

Bayly wasn't sure whether to be insulted or flattered but he didn't say anything. He just kept his eyes on Henderson, whose face was flushed and whose hands acted out his words.

"The way you cover the field, the way you run the bases, the way your uniform gets dirty even on artificial turf. There's something magnetic there for me. And when I watched you suffering through that terrible slump, when I heard how the home fans, those fickle awful people, turned on you, booed you, I knew I had to do something. I knew there was a solution." He paused and looked very proud. "And I was happy to have found it."

"I never did thank you for that."

"Oh yes. Every time you swing the bat you do." He stood and picked up his briefcase. "I hope to see you again soon, Mr. Bayly."

"Call me Jack."

Henderson's gratitude was so childlike that Bayly felt embarrassed for him. "Thank you, Jack," he said and left the bar.

Everyone except Bayly was surprised when Buck Snelgrove didn't show up the next day. None of the other umpires knew where he was. He'd left his hotel to go to the stadium and that was the last anyone had seen of him. The other three men in the crew worked the first game. The day after, a replacement was flown in and stayed for the rest of the series. It wasn't until the fifth inning of the fourth game that Snelgrove was found wandering shoeless through a suburban industrial park. He was unwashed and unshaven and he reported that he'd been forced into a car at gunpoint and blindfolded by somebody wearing a rubber Dracula mask and an old San Francisco Giants cap. He'd been taken to a kind of basement apartment, he'd no idea where it was, and held there for three days. He'd been well fed, but the kidnapper had said nothing to him. A couple of hand written notes, which the kidnapper immediately destroyed, said he was being held until Sunday afternoon and then he would be released unharmed. "The guy even put the ball games on the radio for me," Snelgrove said with amazement.

After the third inning of that day's game, Snelgrove was blindfolded again and taken to the industrial park. He was let off after having his shoes removed and warned not to take off the blindfold until he counted to one thousand.

Bayly's team swept the weekend series. The opponents filed a protest. The Commissioner of Baseball launched an investigation. But, in the end, nothing could be proved.

After the Sunday game, Bayly came out of the players' entrance to a horde of autograph seekers. Among them, waiting patiently for his turn, was Henderson.

"Could I have your autograph, please, Mr. Bayly? It's for my son. He's your biggest fan. Could you make it, To Mike?"

As Bayly wrote his name on the scrap of paper, Henderson whispered, "Great series, Jack."

Without looking up, Bayly said, "Kidnapping's against the law, ain't it?"

"I won't tell if you won't." Then, taking the autograph, he said "Thanks, Mr. Bayly", and vanished into the sea of people.

"I know what your trouble is," Henderson said.

"How did you get my number?" Bayly asked. He was in a foul mood, the latest legal papers from his wife spread all over the kitchen table of his lakeside condo. His wife's settlement demands had gone up to include a share of all Bayly's playing bonuses. And the only calls he was expecting were from his lawyer and from Janine, the woman his wife was claiming as co-respondent in the divorce proceedings.

"It's easier than you think," Henderson answered.

Bayly took a deep breath. After all, Henderson had bailed him out twice. And Bayly had a fat World Series ring on his finger that, way back at the All-Star Break, he never figured he'd see. He guessed he owed the guy a little civility. "So you know what my trouble is this time, do you?"

"Yes, Jack. It's woman trouble, isn't it?"

Bayly laughed. "If I didn't know better, I'd figure you had my phone tapped and a spy satellite hanging around outside my bedroom window."

Henderson joined in with a soft chuckle. "Oh, it's not quite like that, Jack. But I have the root of your problem right here. And I have the solution." Bayly could imagine Henderson patting that briefcase and then tapping his temple.

"I sure appreciate everything you've done for me in the past, buddy. But I don't think you can help me now."

"You'd be surprised, Jack. After all, you're my favourite. And I hate to see you suffer."

"I appreciate your concern, but..."

"I'll be in touch soon, Jack."

Bayly listened to the phone go dead and cradled the receiver. He felt uneasy but didn't know why. He spent another half hour going over the papers. Then he was going to meet his lawyer and head for a showdown with his wife and hers.

He dressed in a suit, something he hated but which lawyers always seemed to demand. Traffic was good and he was early so he decided to make one quick stop. Just for a little boost of courage.

He pulled up in front of Janine's duplex and let himself in. She lived on a busy street that mixed houses with small shops and family-owned restaurants. From the window of the café across the street you could get a good view of Janine's front door. Several patrons saw Jack Bayly go into the building and then re-emerge, his body contorted in grief, his cries of anguish audible even inside the restaurant.

"Jeez," one of the customers said, the cappuccino stopped halfway to his lips," I wonder what his trouble is."

The small, curly haired, bright eyed man at the next table gave a puzzled frown. "I haven't the slightest idea," he said.

Avenging Miriam

Originally published in a slightly different form in *Ellery Queen Mystery Magazine*, December 2001
Winner of the 2001 Ellery Queen Readers Award

"'I JUST WANT TO PUT IT BEHIND ME AND GET ON WITH MY life.' That's what one of them said." He handed the paper to Kieran who read the first few paragraphs of the article and saw the quote for himself.

"I must confess, I find the cold-bloodedness of that even more incomprehensible now than when I first read it," Sebastian said. "Imagine. Saying something like that, as if she had failed a math test or dented her father's car, instead of murdering another fourteen-year-old girl."

To Kieran, it did seem cynical. "What's this to do with me?" He handed back the clipping.

"The killers are all young offenders," Sebastian said, "They'll do three years at most. They'll be out in time to apply for their first driver's licenses or attend their high school graduations. That doesn't seem fair. So I want to hire you."

"To kill that girl?" He pointed at the article.

"To kill them all."

There were nine in the group of children who had beaten a schoolmate to death one evening after dinner, while other kids were taking piano lessons or hanging at the mall.

"I'm sorry to disappoint you, but I'm not your man," Kieran said. "I don't kill children, for money or otherwise."

Sebastian shook his head. "Don't be fooled by acne and braces and innocent looks. Children don't slaughter their peers. Chronologically they may be fourteen or fifteen, but they're not children, I assure you. They're monsters."

"That may be, but I won't execute them for you." Kieran sipped his coffee. "What's your interest? You the father? Uncle? What?"

"I'm not related to Miriam. I'm just a concerned citizen who can see when a gross injustice is being committed and who has the wherewithal to do something about it."

"You're more noble than I am. I'm not your man."

As if he hadn't heard, Sebastian took a folded sheet of paper from an inside jacket pocket and held it out. "This is a list of their names and addresses."

Kieran didn't take the paper, but Sebastian did not withdraw it. Eventually Kieran reached out. Once the sheet was in his hand, he did not open it. "You shouldn't have this," he said. Under the law, the names of young offenders could not be made public.

"Legally, true. But you know as well as I do, every time there's a case such as this, people in the community know. It's not hard to learn who the culprits are."

Kieran unfolded the sheet. Miriam's name was at the top, then the identities of her killers. Each name and address was typed in Helvetica on a single line, double-spaced. There was nothing in the way the words looked to give any hint of what the people behind them had done: Adam, Rebecca, Tiffany, one common or artificial name after another.

Kieran scanned the list. He read it again slowly, and then more slowly still. His sadness must have shown.

"It's an awful thing, but some crimes are too great to be ignored. When you have the power to make a difference and don't, aren't you an accessory? I always felt so. Do you have children?"

Kieran did not discuss his personal life with clients, but this felt different. "I have two daughters." He had not seen the girls in years, his occupation driving a wedge between him and their mother.

"Unpalatable as this might be, before you make a decision, think about one of your daughters in Miriam's place."

Kieran tried to imagine what it must have been like for the murdered girl. The incomprehension when the gang turned on her. They were people she thought of as friends; who she wanted to be like and to impress. Why were they doing this? The question must have loomed so large in her mind that she didn't feel the blows at first, their existence numbing her to the pain they caused.

Then terror must have set in. Surrounded, driven to the ground, blows from fists and open hands turning to dehumanizing kicks. The expensive cross trainers and the Docs and the trendy hiking shoes slamming into her body as she squirmed, trying to find escape. But there were nine of them, so it was easy to surround her. No matter where she put her hands to ward off the blows, most of her body was left unprotected. For every kick deflected, eight others found their mark. She cried and begged, but mercy was not forthcoming. At some point, one of them, her leg growing tired, picked up a stick and used that to beat Miriam on the head and neck.

Did they talk to her, Kieran wondered, as they were killing her? Did they explain to her why? Did they call her names and abuse her with their mouths as well as their limbs? Did they hurl accusations and condemn her family? Did they laugh?

Then, for a moment, they had stopped. All nine of them had stepped back and let her rise painfully to her feet. They were letting her go. She was bleeding and stunned and every step was painful but they let her stagger away. How did she feel then, as hope soared inside her? Did she thank them? Did she thank some god for making them stop? Or did she just move as quickly as she could, urging on her unsteady legs, wondering what she would tell her parents. How she would explain to her teachers why her homework was not done.

In the end, none of that mattered. She hadn't gone fifty feet before they set on her again. That, to Kieran, was the cruelest part; letting hope build and then grinding it out. They beat her and kicked her and finally left her lying on the bank of a small creek where she died.

Kieran shook his head. It was senseless. He couldn't conceive of such behaviour. He placed the paper against his lips, shut his eyes and considered for some time.

"All right," he said at length. "I'm your man."

Sebastian smiled. "I know this is a huge undertaking. Thank you for doing the right thing."

"It's business," Kieran said.

"I don't imagine there's a volume discount."

Kieran shook his head. "In fact, there's a volume premium. Nine random people, you'd get a break. But nine kids all linked to the same event, the cops are going to know what's up from the word Go. That adds a whole whack of danger pay. You fine with that?"

"This has to be done, and it has to be done right. As my grandfather used to say, 'The craftsman is worthy of his hire'."

"Yes," Kieran said, "I'm worthy all right."

Kieran explained that Sebastian would have to be patient. The first of the killers would die quickly. The rest would be on guard then, as would the authorities, so Kieran would have to wait for them to relax again, and begin to forget that there was someone in the dark, waiting.

"The wheels of justice grind slow," Sebastian said. "But they grind fine. I'm confident that the job will be done to my satisfaction. Time is not of the essence." He handed Kieran a manila envelope. "Photos of the monsters," he said.

Kieran drove to Vancouver. He was tired when he arrived but, instead of going to his hotel, he went to the airport and left his car in long-term parking. People tended to notice out-of-province plates on the street. He took a bus downtown, checked in to a mid-range hotel and had a nap.

He killed the first three the next night. This had not been his plan. He'd anticipated spending a few days scouting the situation and working out the most efficient and least risky way of picking them off one by one. But then, as he cruised past the home of one of the female killers, the door opened and she stepped outside. Kieran followed her discreetly. It wasn't difficult. The car he'd rented was not distinctive and the quarry, like so many teenagers, was oblivious to everything that was not of direct concern to her.

She made two stops on her trip, meeting two young men who Kieran recognized as other members of the group. It was better than he had hoped. They were together, in clear violation of their probation. Better yet, they headed straight for the centre of Stanley Park to blaze. Kieran followed and they were all dead before the bong went around once. He dragged their bodies into the bushes. They might be discovered first thing in the morning by a jogger, or they could lie undisturbed for days. Kieran hoped for the latter, but planned on the former.

Driving back over the Burrard Bridge, Kieran thought about what had happened. He hadn't said a word to the kids. He'd just dropped them as cleanly and as quickly as possible. In the instant between life and death he doubted if they made any connection with what was happening to them and what they had done to the girl by the side of a rubbish-choked creek. He'd heard that, at the point of dying, your life flashes before your eyes. If that were true, did the lives of those three young killers freeze-frame on their viciousness and cause the truth to make them think, "Oh, so *this* is why we're being killed. I guess there is justice after all"? Kieran doubted it. He decided then that the rest of the condemned would know why.

Kieran requested a smoking room. He took out the photos of the dead and burned them. They were high school yearbook photos and the bland artlessness and frozen smiles gave no hint of rage inside. He wondered what the old scientists who felt you could distinguish a criminal by his face would have made of these images. He held each photo in turn over an ashtray and watched as the flames melted the photographic paper, twisting the faces grotesquely, making them look truly monstrous. He held on and watched until the flames licked his fingers. When all three were done, he emptied the ashtray in the toilet and flushed.

The next morning, there was nothing in the papers about three bodies found in Stanley Park. Nor was there anything about three missing teens. Maybe they were frequently out all night, so no one was concerned yet.

Whatever the reason, Kieran had a chance to get further ahead than he had envisaged. He went over the list while sitting at an outdoor cafe and chose a boy named Christopher. He found it difficult to work up much enthusiasm for executing the girls.

Christopher's family had moved away from the neighbourhood where most of the others still lived. They had settled in the suburb of Burnaby, perhaps thinking they could escape the notoriety, the stares and the whispers. But Burnaby was not so far. And the reality, as Kieran knew, was that you can't leave the past behind. Try as you might, it will find you and bring you pain.

Kieran found the new address and scouted the area thoroughly. Then he went to a nearby mall and waited in the Food Court. He ate Indian, drank coffee and watched the kids who gathered, any of them capable of anything.

He scrutinized the faces and realized with surprise that Christopher was there, laughing with a new gang of friends. Kieran hadn't expected it to be so simple.

An hour later the boy left in the company of a few companions. Kieran wondered if they would head straight home or stop in a desolate spot and slaughter one of their number.

They set off in a 4x4. Kieran followed as the driver let passengers off along the route. When Christopher got out at the top of a flight of steps that led into a ravine, Kieran knew that the boy would have to follow the path that led across a small footbridge, then climb the hill to the street where his house stood.

Kieran drove as quickly as the speed limit allowed and parked near the exit of the ravine. He walked in, pistol in his jacket pocket, and reached the footbridge ahead of Christopher. Kieran had just crossed the bridge when he recognized the figure coming towards him. Christopher must have seen Kieran at the same moment, for he took two or three more faltering steps and then stopped. Kieran kept walking. Christopher took a step back, then two, but he was still gazing into the gloom, trying to figure out if he should stand his ground or flee.

Kieran said, "Hi, Chris," in a friendly voice.

The familiarity froze Christopher. Who was this who knew his name but who he was sure he did not recognize? The same soft voice said, "Miriam says hello." Then Christopher knew the only smart thing to do was to run.

Christopher was lean and his legs were long. Under other circumstances, he could far outpace a middle-aged man. But he was wearing his jeans pulled low around his hips, showing boxer shorts. As he ran his pants began to slip down. He stumbled, trying to wrestle them higher while fleeing. His pants were reluctant to move but the boy was unwilling to stop and do the job properly. He kept on his erratic pace, turning his head frequently to watch in panic the man who followed him. Then he tripped on a root, perhaps, or an unevenness of ground. He fell abruptly and hard. He made one abortive attempt to get up, but his need caused him to fail. Then the boy began crawling, scrambling along the dirt path, weeping and sniffling. Kieran caught up with him. He looked down at the boy half-curled on the ground, his hands about his head, making noises of pleading.

It would have been easy to have shot him and left immediately. But Kieran thought about the first three and how none of them knew why they died. This one was going to know, just as his family would know, as soon as his three dead friends were found. They'd know that their son had not been killed in a random act of violence. Not the way Miriam died, but because Miriam died. That made Kieran wonder what Christopher's mother thought of her son when she looked at him across the breakfast table, knowing about him what she knew.

Kieran crouched next to the prone youth. "Sit up," he said. "We're going to have a chat." Tentatively, the boy shifted one of his arms from over his eyes and peered at Kieran. Uncertain at first, and then with growing hope, he rose to his knees, sniffled and wiped his eyes with his sleeve. His lip quivered. "Don't kill me," he said. "Please."

Kieran indicated a tree with the barrel of his gun. "Sit," he said.

The boy leaned his back against the tree and stared at the gun. "Please."

"Is that what she said as you were killing her? How many times, I wonder? After the first couple, it must have become easier to ignore."

The boy started to cry again. Kieran waited until the weeping subsided. "Why did you do it?"

The boy shook his head. "I don't know. I don't know why."

"Because other people were doing it? Or did you start it? Was it planned out in advance? Or was it something that just happened?"

"I don't know. I was just there."

Kieran wondered what the truth was. Had there been a phone tree? "Hi, it's Tracy. Whatcha doin' tonight? You wanna get together? We're gonna, like, go grab a latte, check out this new club and, then, like, beat Miriam to death. Yeah, I think it sounds cool. Call Mike and ask him to tell Lindsay. Oh and you know that new zit cream? Does it, like, work any good?" He hoped it hadn't been like that, but with kids these days you never knew.

"Wearing your pants like that makes it tough to run, doesn't it? You know why you wear your pants like that? I bet you don't have a clue. It's a gang thing from LA. The gangs started wearing their pants baggy in the crotch so they could hide weapons. If you'd had a weapon hidden in there you might not be in the predicament you're currently facing."

The boy sobbed harder. Kieran began to feel uneasy. He didn't want to stay too long. "Listen," he said, "I'm going to teach you another valuable lesson. You know why this is happening, right?"

The kid looked scared and blank and shook his head, wiping his nose on his sleeve again. "Miriam," Kieran said. The kid started to wail more loudly.

Kieran decided there was little point in dragging things out. "Here's the lesson. Most teenage kids think they're invincible, that they're going to live forever. If they understood and embraced their own mortality, they'd be better off I think. They'd be more empathetic. Make more constructive use of their time. So I'm helping you realize your mortality right now. This is a valuable life lesson; one of the secrets of the universe. You're lucky. Not many young people get to die with such clarity of mind." Then Kieran put the pistol away. Christopher stared in disbelief, as if he could smell mercy. Until, considering the surrounding neighbourhood, Kieran reached into another pocket and took out a guitar string.

• • • •

Kieran stayed in Vancouver a few more days. By then all four bodies had been found. Nothing was mentioned in the papers about the connection between them. But the cops would have linked them instantly and the rest of the targets would drop out of sight. There'd be no more opportunity in the immediate future. There was, however, one stop Kieran could make on the way home.

Just like Christopher's parents, Rachel's mother thought she could run away from trouble. She had taken her daughter to stay with relatives in Calgary. Further than Burnaby, but still not far enough.

Sebastian supplied him with the new address, the names of the people with whom Rachel and her mother were staying, the phone number. He even provided Kieran with a new photograph of the girl, who had cut and dyed her hair. The photo was taken on the street, showing her in company with an older woman. Kieran studied the girl briefly and then focused on the mother. She was perhaps forty, attractive, with lines that gave her face character and depth. He studied the face for a considerable time.

Kieran went to the airport and got his car. The rate they charged for parking was usurious, but he reckoned Sebastian could afford it.

In Calgary, Kieran drove to Rachel's cousin's place. It was a typical sub-division house, rather ugly, squatting behind a bloated two-car garage. There was a mini-van in the driveway and a sprinkler on the lawn. There was no sign of life. He came back that evening and watched briefly. Lights burned in the windows and he saw silhouetted figures moving behind sheer curtains, but no one came out.

He drove past the local schools until he found the high school he suspected Rachel would be attending. Then he went downtown for dinner.

Since he was in Alberta, he had a steak while he tried to think of a plan to kill Rachel, but his thoughts kept drifting. He was distracted by snatches of conversation from other tables. He found himself watching female patrons and waitresses as they breezed past. The image of Rachel's mother kept crowding into his head. It wasn't just that the mother was attractive to him. It was seeing them together, mother and daughter so much alike, in a photo where they looked happy and ordinary. But when he looked at them, together and smiling, he wondered what she thought of her daughter now. How did she rationalize the enormity of the crime? He wanted to ask her. He knew it was time to go home.

The next morning he started driving east. He'd let things cool off over the winter and finish in the spring. All the way home, across a thousand miles of prairie and through the vast northern woods, thoughts of Rachel's mother kept him company.

"We're certainly off to a flying start," Sebastian said. "Five down, four to go."

Kieran hadn't been paying much attention. It took a while before the words sank in. Three in the park. One in the ravine. Four, no matter how you add it up. "Five?"

"I guess you haven't read this." He handed Kieran a newspaper clipping from the *Calgary Herald*, dated the day after Kieran left town. Rachel's body had been found in her room. She had taken an overdose.

"Her mother's pills?" Kieran asked.

Sebastian shook his head. "They were her own. She'd been having trouble sleeping, apparently. Nightmares. I can't imagine why."

No mention was made of bad dreams in the article, nor of what might have caused them. Nothing in the brief piece indicated that this was anything other than another sad teenage suicide.

Sebastian said, "She was also having trouble at her new school. She didn't fit in and I understand she was picked on a lot. What goes around comes around, I suppose. I don't suppose there's a rebate for this one."

"You can ask," Kieran said.

Sebastian chuckled. "Well, hearing about the deaths of her friends must have helped nudge her along. So I guess you can take partial credit anyway."

Kieran monitored the West Coast media and when the four killings of the previous autumn had not been mentioned for three months, it was time to go back. He took the train, booking a stopover in Calgary.

It was not difficult to find Rachel's mother. She no longer lived in the house he had watched in the fall. She had recently purchased a modest condominium in a residential area near the downtown core.

As he observed her for several days, her habits fell into a regular pattern. Her routine included having lunch most days in one of the same three restaurants with the same individual co-workers or the same small knot of people. He was struck by the ordinariness of it and marvelled at the tenacity that kept people going in such tedious circumstances.

After work she rarely went out with anyone. She stayed in or walked to a small pub a few blocks from home. She would sit at a table for two against the back wall. There was a sconce beside the table in which two flame-shaped bulbs burned dimly. By this light, she would read a book while nursing a glass of red wine. She never had more than one glass and she never stayed longer than an hour.

Kieran was glad that she didn't sit at the bar. Women sitting alone on bar stools struck him as tragic.

Rachel's mother read slowly and occasionally flipped back a page, presumably to pick up a line or a thought that she had missed. Kieran watched her surreptitiously for the first few nights. He sat in a different place each evening. One night he watched a hockey game on the TV behind the bar. One night he did the crossword in the *Globe & Mail*. One night he read a book of his own.

After almost two weeks, Kieran approached her. She had just sat down and the waitress had not come to take her order. "Excuse me," he said. "I was wondering if I could buy you a drink."

She looked up at him intently and did not respond right away.

"I'm not trying to pick you up or anything," he said. "I just admire anyone who reads Dickens." He indicated her copy of *Oliver Twist* on the table and then held up the *Bleak House* he had been pretending to read for the last few evenings.

Seated opposite her, he ordered each of them a glass of red wine. "Do you live near here?" she asked.

"No. I'm just in town on business. My hotel's close by."

"Which one?"

"Journey's End."

She nodded. "Where are you from?"

"Toronto now," he said. "But I'm from Vancouver originally."

Her face brightened. "Really? That's where I'm from."

"No kidding. What a coincidence. How long you been here?"

What she told him was mostly the truth, based on what he knew of her life, and she willingly accepted the carefully constructed story he presented as reality.

"I don't want you to get the wrong impression," he said, "but I've been in here a few nights and I couldn't help notice you."

She looked at him as if expecting the advance to come now.

"You must like it here," was all he said.

She smiled. "It gets me out of the house."

"Lots of things do that. You could take up yoga or join a book club. You like to read."

"I don't feel very social a lot of the time."

"It's none of my business, but you look kind of sad. Anything you'd care to discuss with a stranger you're never going to see again?"

"How can you be sure of that?"

"I'm forty-two years old and I've never been to Calgary before in my life. It's a fluke I'm here now. I had to cover for somebody who got sick. The odds of our meeting again are extremely long. So, is there anything you want to talk about?"

She shook her head. "Not really. Do you have any kids?"

"Two," Kieran said. "Daughters. They live with their mother. How about you?"

"I had a daughter, too."

"Had?"

Rachel's mother shook her head. "She died last spring."

"I'm terribly sorry. I didn't mean to stir up bad memories."

"It's all right. Everything stirs up bad memories. You didn't know."

They sat in silence, Kieran studying the woman's face while she relived the memories unspooling in her head. "What work do you do?" he asked softly.

She looked in his eyes and smiled. "You don't have to change the subject," she said. "I don't mind talking about it."

"I figured, because you just said..."

"I lied. I want to talk about it but I try to keep myself under control. That's why I come to this place. Nobody here talks to me about anything. I think my friends are tired of hearing about it, not that I have that many friends here, so I try to hide. But it doesn't always work. Rachel killed herself."

Kieran let out his breath slowly. "I can't imagine what that must be like," he said. "Losing a child that way."

"You know, it's been almost a year and I still can't imagine it either."

"Was there something specific that happened? Had there been any signs?"

Rachel's mother looked down at the table again. Her hands played with the stem of her glass and then began riffling the pages of her book. "No," she said. "There'd been some trouble back in Vancouver. She got involved with some bad kids. I tried to tell her, but how many fourteen year olds listen to their mothers? I brought her here thinking we could leave the trouble behind."

"I guess trouble has a way of following you around."

"Sad but true."

"Things didn't change when you got here?"

"For a bit. A few weeks. A month. Just until she got settled in a little and found the kids here who were just like the kids at home. And then it was like nothing was any different."

"How did she behave?"

"I don't know. She'd do things out of spite. She used to hitchhike to school. This started just before she turned thirteen. I'd tell her not to do it, but she'd leave the house in the morning and when I'd leave for work I'd see her a block away, standing by the side of the road with her thumb out. She'd stare right at me, like a challenge. There must have been things I could have done better, but for the life of me I don't know what they are."

She sipped her wine and Kieran remained silent. She had more to say yet, and she wasn't after his opinion.

"When I used to see kids on the street, I thought that they all left home because they were beaten or abused. I realize now how naive I was. Some of those kids were just like Rachel. There was nothing awful going on at home. Nothing unusual, anyway. They just left. They skipped school. They ran away. She used to tell me that she was spending the night at this friend's house, or that one's. Those other kids must have told their parents the same thing, I suppose. But they never spent the night at anyone's house. Sometimes they'd sleep in apartment building stairwells. Why? What was the reason?"

"It must have been difficult for you."

She shrugged. "It had its moments. You know what the hardest thing is? I have so many questions for her that nobody will ever be able to answer. Even if they could, I don't imagine I'd accept them because I don't think I could understand."

"It sounds like she was pretty lost."

"Yes. That's what hurts. I never saw the amount of pain she must have been in." Rachel's mother raised her face and held her chin forward bravely. "She was a good girl. Really she was."

Kieran imagined one of the pictures of the murdered girl, her head in the creek, face down, hair matted. Her body bruised and bleeding from the ferocity of her attackers. He felt the urge to tell Rachel's mother that, despite what she might say, good girls didn't do that to other children. He restrained himself. "I'm sure she was a good girl," he said. "I guess it's just that everybody's got conflicts. Everybody's confused at least some of the time."

Rachel's mother was silent. "I'm sorry," Kieran said finally. He was tired of talking about it, even if she wasn't. "This is a bit of a downer. I really didn't mean to dredge up so much."

She made a dismissive gesture. "Most days, it doesn't take much dredging."

"Would you like to get something to eat?" he asked.

Kieran took the train the rest of the way to Vancouver the next afternoon. Much of the way, he thought about his time with Rachel's mother. It hadn't been entirely satisfying. He'd never felt the moment was right to ask directly most of the questions he had, and he hadn't been able to divine the answers indirectly. But he had a job to do. He forced the disappointment aside and tried to focus.

He dispatched the first three of the four remaining killers over two nights. The third one was dead before the first two bodies had been found, before panic among the families could erupt again, before the police could go back on alert. The waiting had proven wise. The targets were careless and obviously considered themselves beyond the reach of vengeance.

They all cried. One of them said that it wasn't his fault, that the other kids forced him to do it. One claimed he hadn't done anything at all, just watched. Kieran explained how, if that were true, it was worse than taking part. The third one pleaded for mercy because he was only fifteen. "Well," Kieran said, "look on the bright side. You got one more year than Miriam did."

There was one left. Kieran's opportunity came two days later. She was walking home from a movie when Kieran pulled up beside her, got out and opened the passenger door. "Get in," he said.

He wasn't sure that she wouldn't scream and run, but she didn't. She looked at him saying nothing, making no move, while he waited by the open door. He could almost feel her thinking. Then she started toward the car. He wondered, as she climbed in and he shut the door, if she used to hitchhike like Rachel and was used to getting into strange vehicles.

When he was behind the wheel, he said, "For a minute there, I wasn't sure what you were going to do."

She shrugged. "I thought about taking off. But you'd have chased me, right?"

"Yes, I'd have come after you."

"I've always known that eventually you would," she said.

"So you know why I'm here."

"Yeah. I've just been wondering *when* you'd get here," she said.

"I spent some time with Rachel's mother." He felt a need to explain, as if the delay had inconvenienced the girl.

She looked surprised. "Why? How do you know Rachel's mom? Rachel killed herself."

He nodded, answering her first question, ignoring the second. "I wanted to try to find out why she did it, and find out how her mother felt about it." He pulled away from the curb.

"I'll tell you why she did it. Because there was this bogeyman out there, coming around at night to kill her, just like he killed all her friends."

"That may be part of it." He felt calm. "Do you suppose it might have been because she felt badly about what she'd done?"

The girl opened her purse and pulled out a pack of cigarettes. The rental car was non-smoking but it seemed to Kieran that it would be petty to stop her. She lit up and blew out a great plume. "I was getting scared waiting for you."

"Oh?"

"I was afraid you wouldn't show."

"There was no need to fear that," he said.

They drove in silence for several minutes before she asked, "Why do you think this has been happening?" There was a plaintive note in her voice. "Why has someone killed all my friends? What did they do to deserve that?"

"Maybe it wasn't what they did but how they did it, and why."

"What the hell does that mean?"

"What did Miriam do to deserve to die?"

She crossed her arms and turned to face out the side window. "You wouldn't understand."

"You could try me."

"Does everybody die for good reasons? Do you ever really know why you're doing it?"

"Sometimes," he said.

"Yeah, right. I don't want to talk about this anymore."

He ignored her. "It should have been quick," he said. "Abrupt, sudden, painless. Not dragged out. I bet she didn't even know why it was happening?"

"So you've never done that? You've never prolonged the agony?"

"No. I've never done it," he said, "unless it was to make sure that the person understood clearly why he was dying. Did Miriam have that understanding, do you suppose?"

The girl shrugged. "She probably knew she was going to die because nobody liked her. Would that be enough reason for you?"

He didn't answer. He had driven to an isolated industrial area of warehouses and small manufacturing facilities. He stopped the car.

She looked at the surroundings, then at him. "I must be stupid," she said. "I was relieved to see you." Kieran figured the details had fallen into place. "You knew about Rachel. You know about everything that's been going on. You're not here to protect me."

"I'm afraid not," he said. He took out the pistol and brought it to bear. It was not as steady as it had been every time before.

She looked at her cigarette and laughed bitterly. "My last smoke and I didn't even take the time to appreciate it." She ground the butt out on the dashboard with sharp, angry motions. "Do I get any last words?"

He released the safety on the pistol.

She said, "You're kidding yourself, you know, if you think you don't do what we did. You've tortured us for months. We couldn't sleep. Afraid to go out. Waiting for you to show up. How many of us got the value of your wisdom before you blew our fucking brains out?"

"Are you finished?" he asked. It took all his energy to focus on the pistol, to keep it steady and aimed true.

"That's up to you, isn't it?" It was warm and close in the confined space. "So," she said, turning in the seat to face him, "what are you going to do now, Dad?"